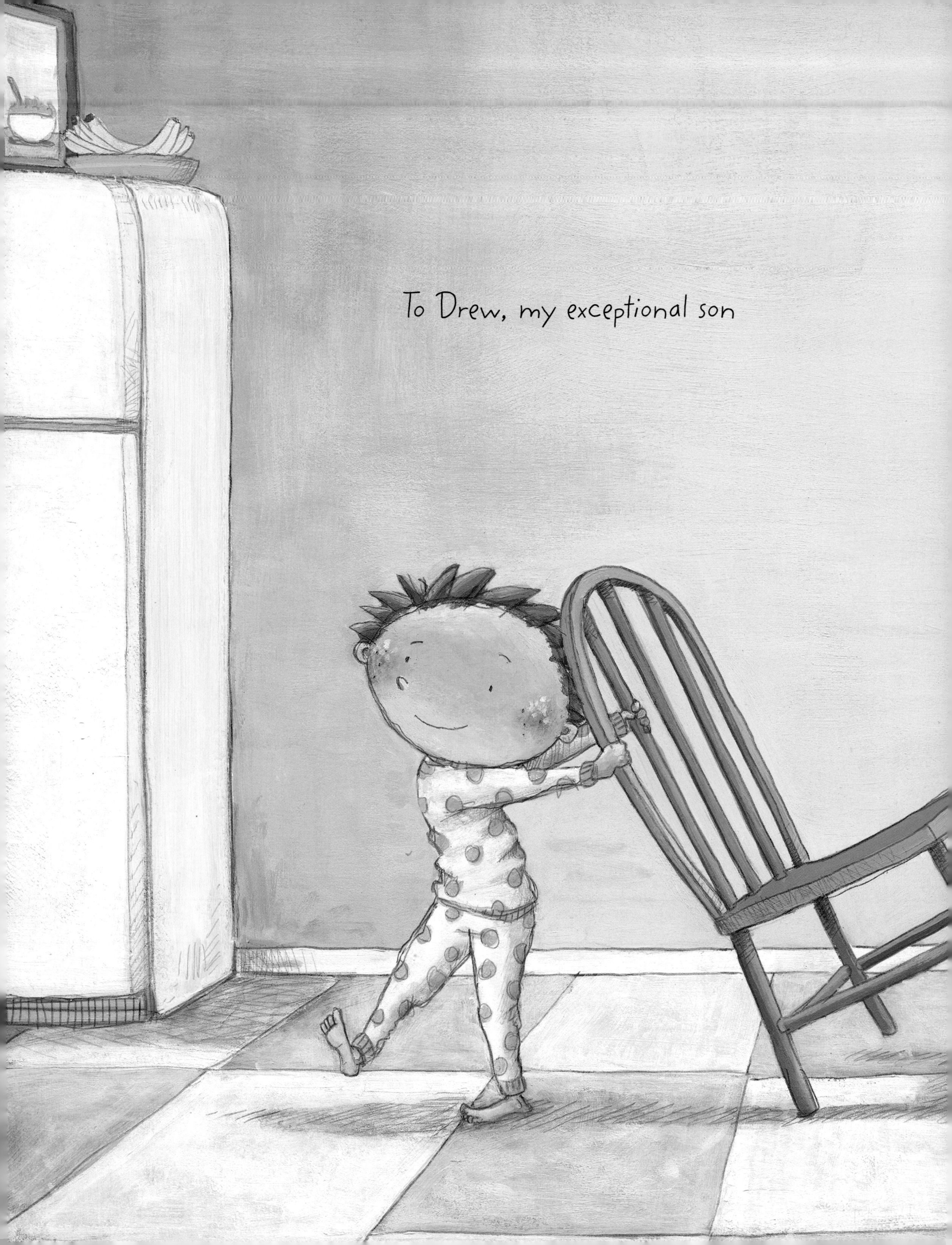

To Drew, my exceptional son

Because

Richard Torrey

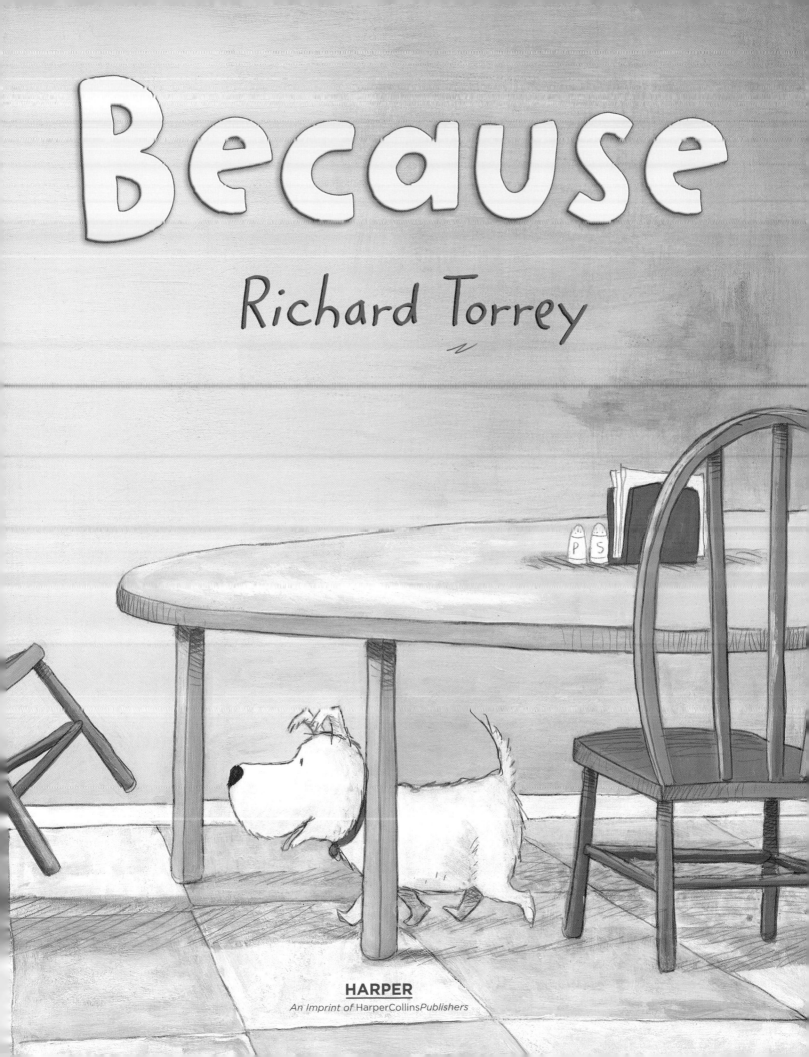

HARPER

An Imprint of HarperCollinsPublishers

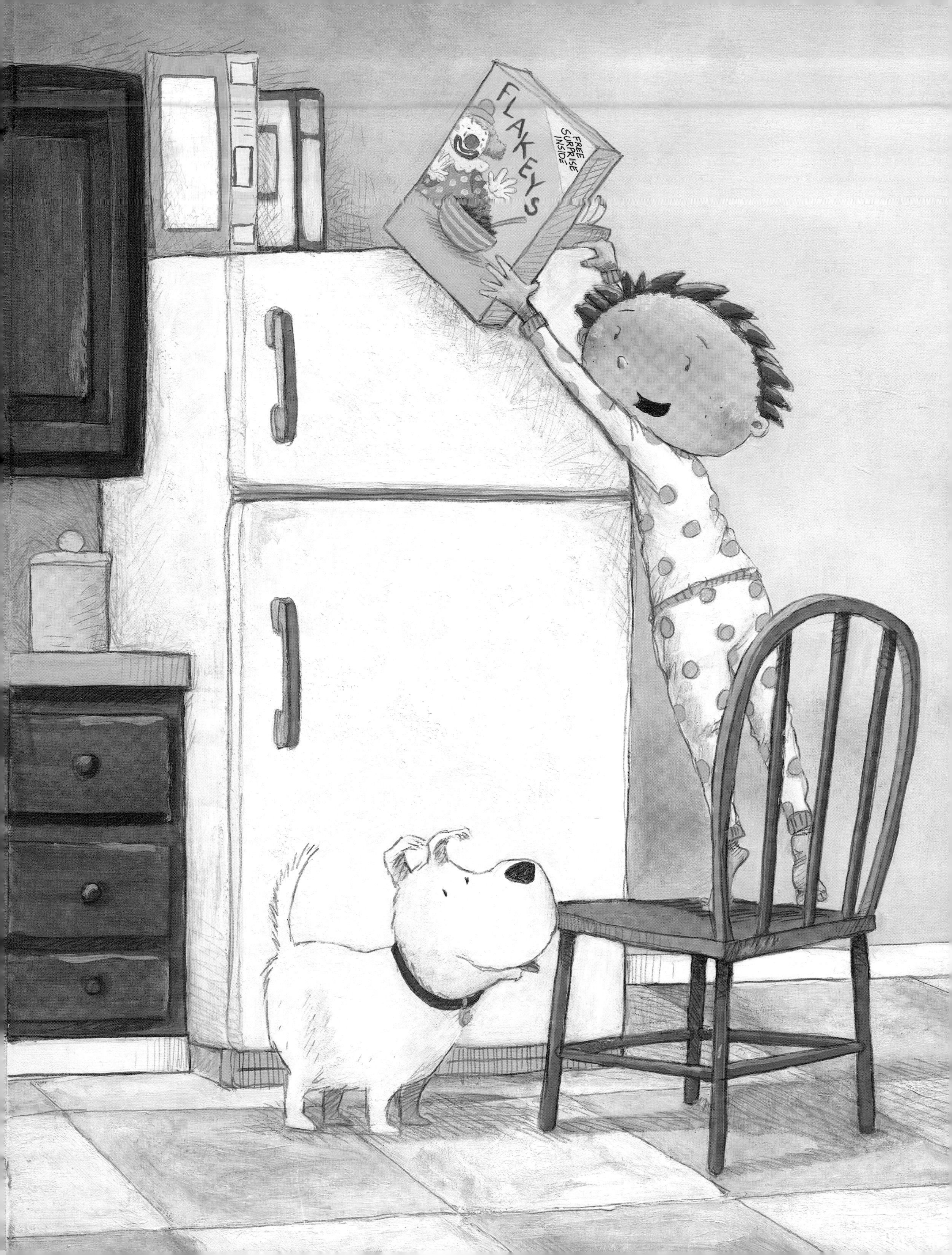
FLAKEYS
FREE SURPRISE INSIDE

My mom says "because" is not a real answer. But I think it is.

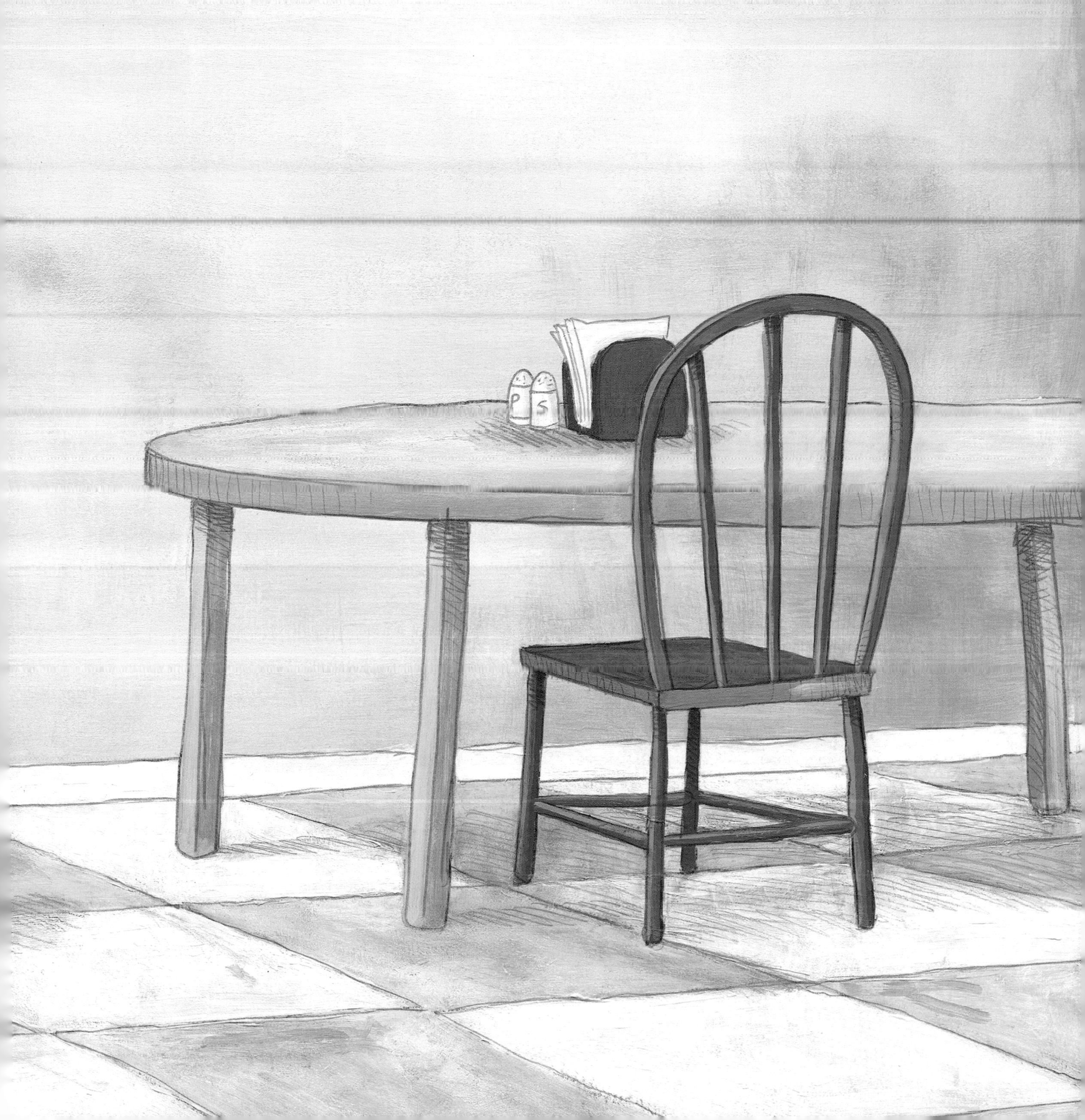
P
S

Because *this* was in it!

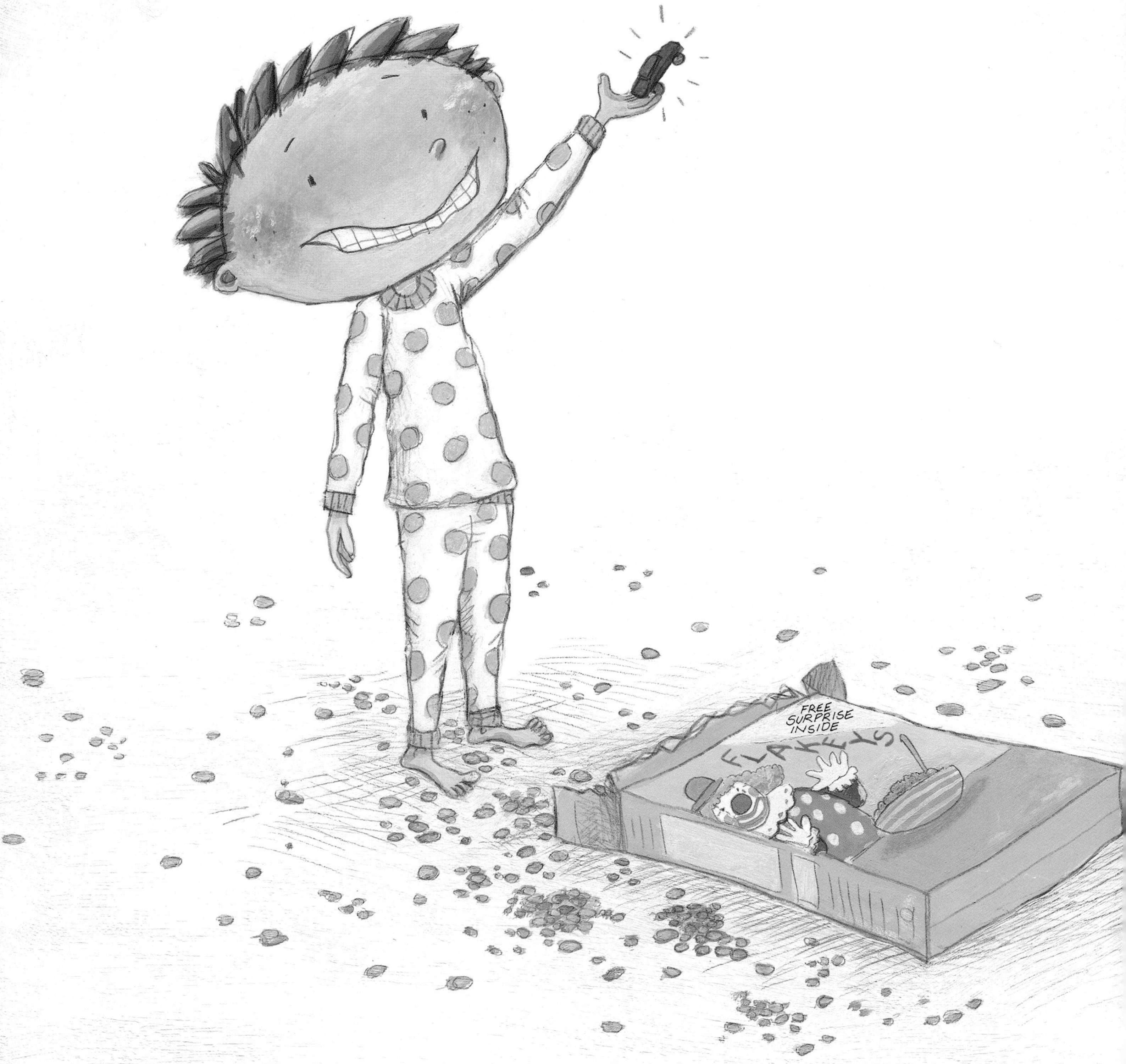
FREE SURPRISE INSIDE
FLAKEYS

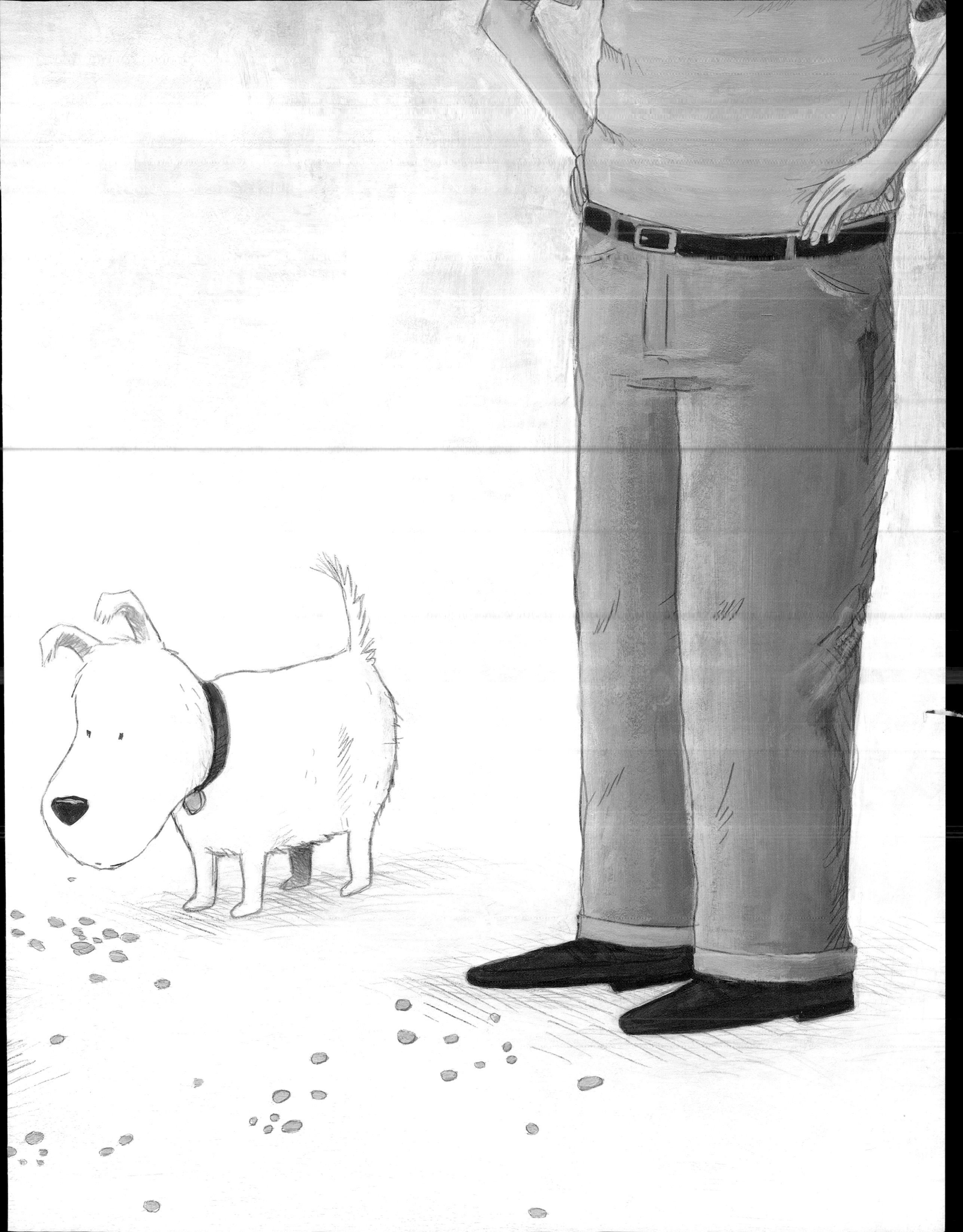

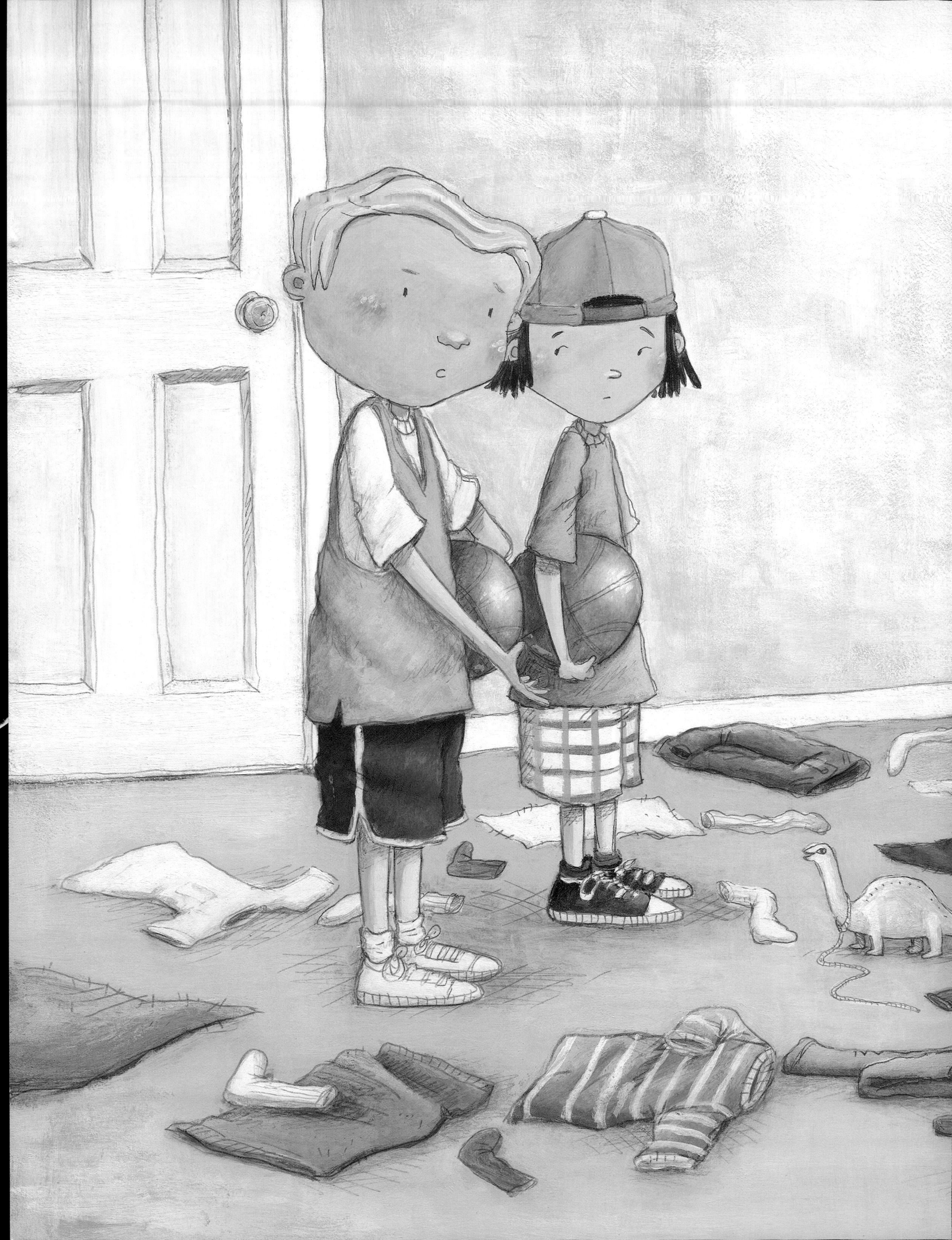

Because it's my spaceship.

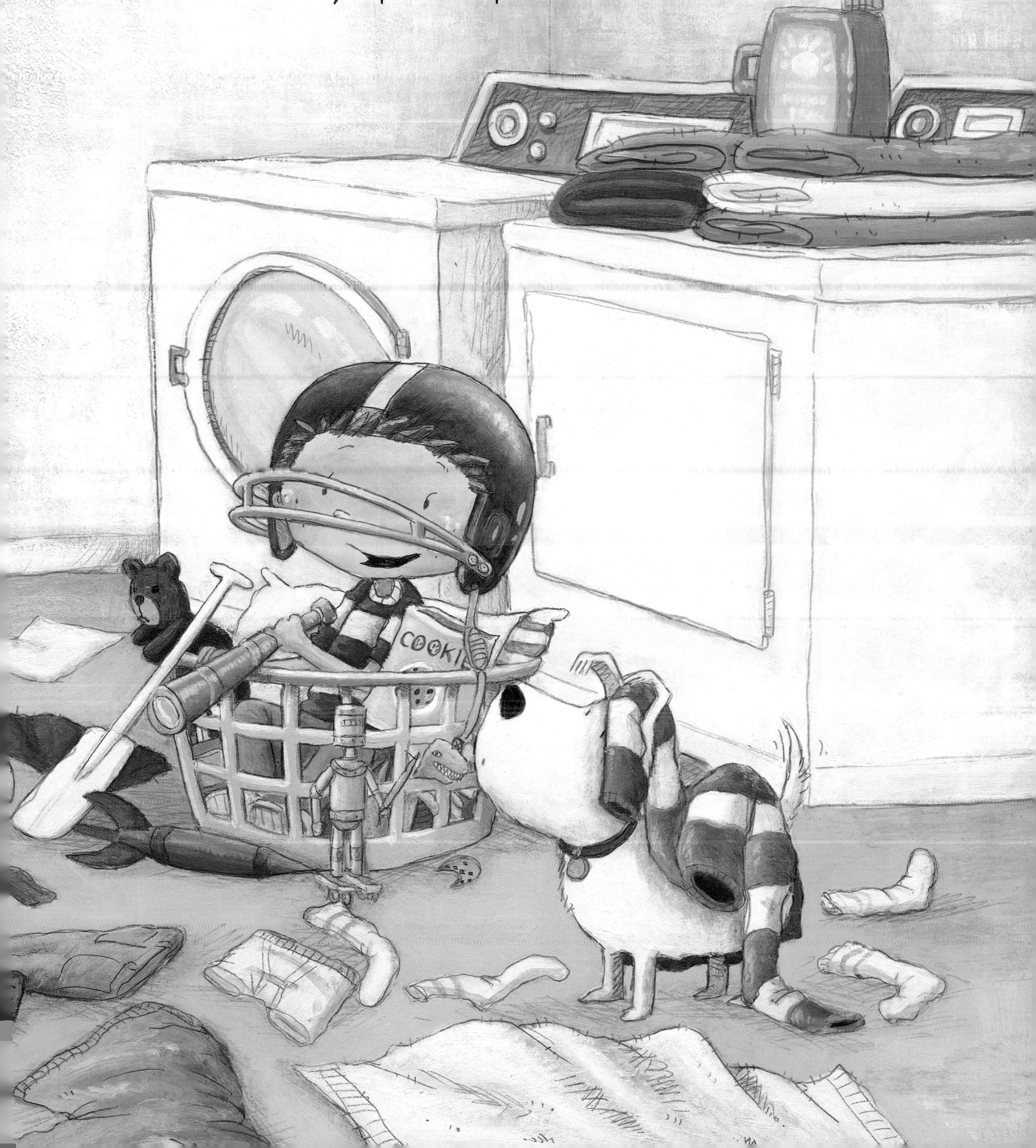
COOKI

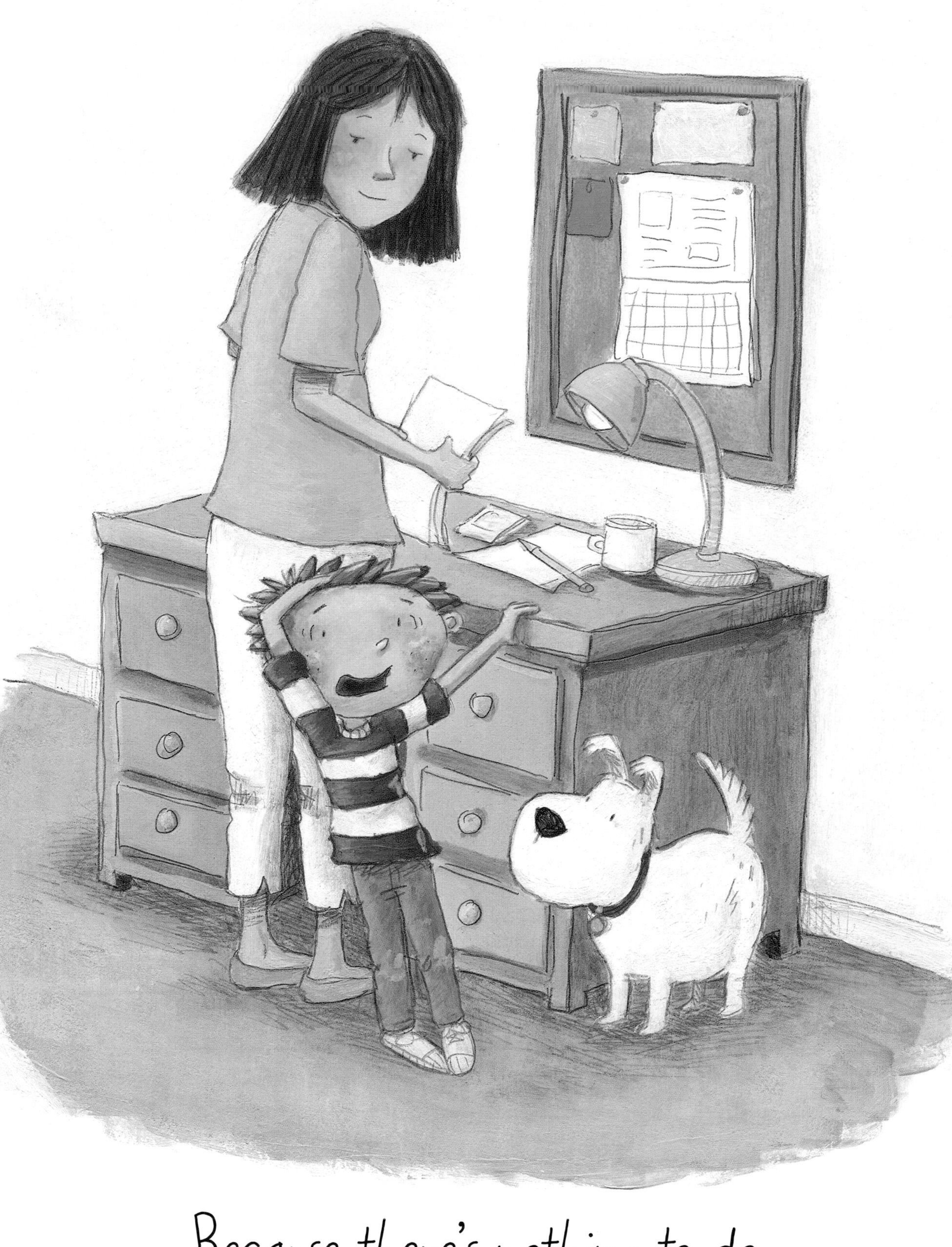

Because there's nothing to do.

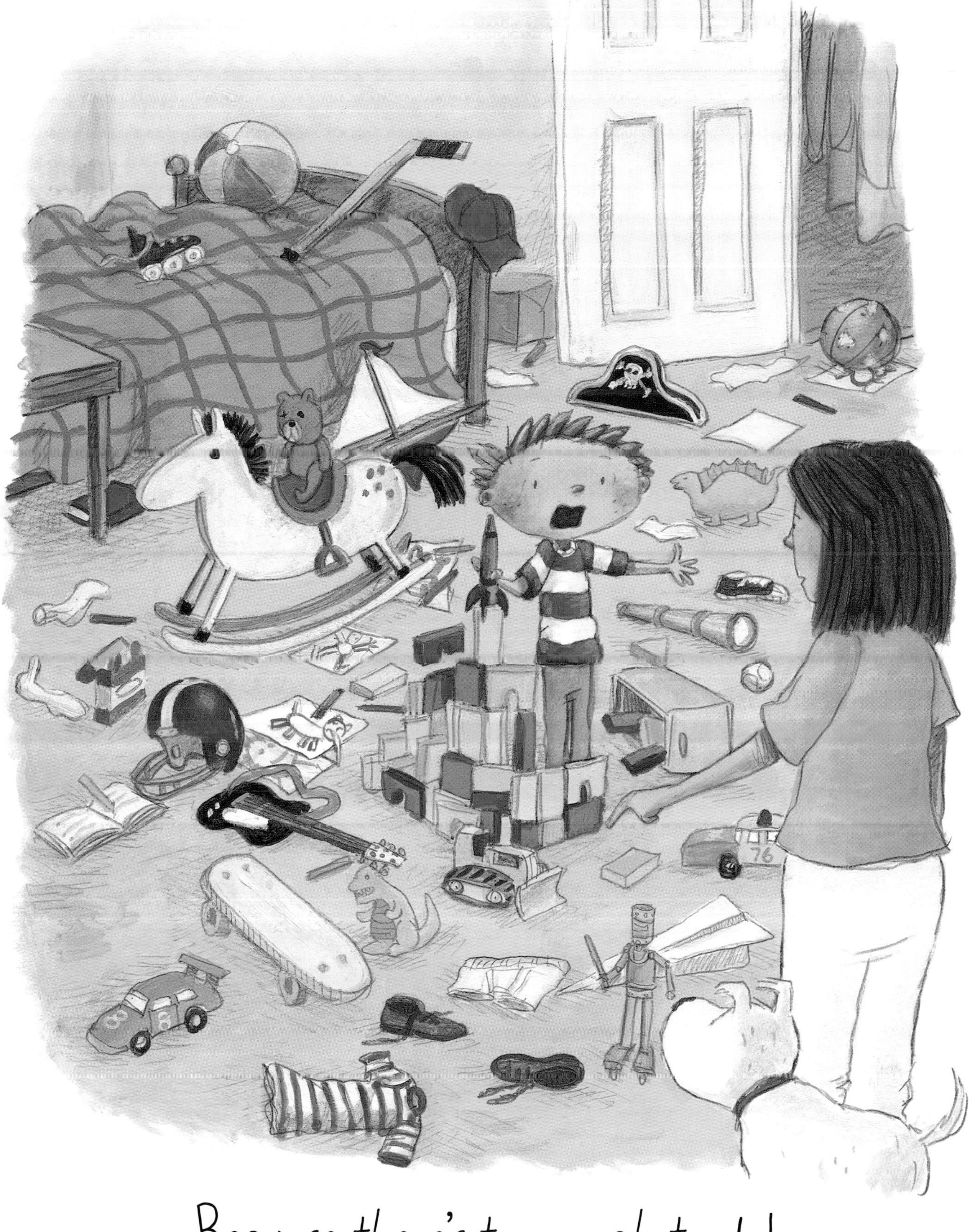
76

Because there's too much to do!

Because you cheated.

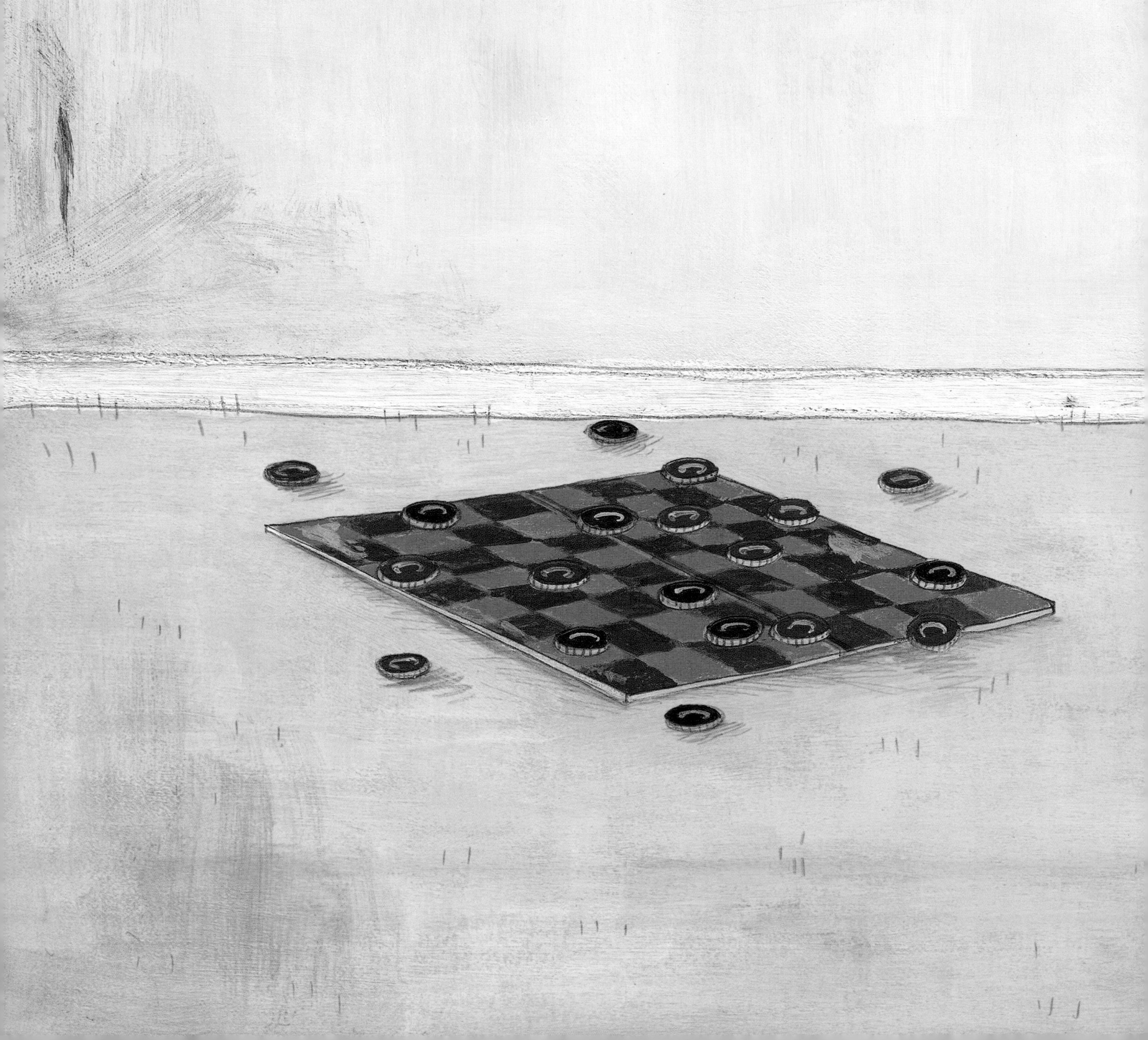

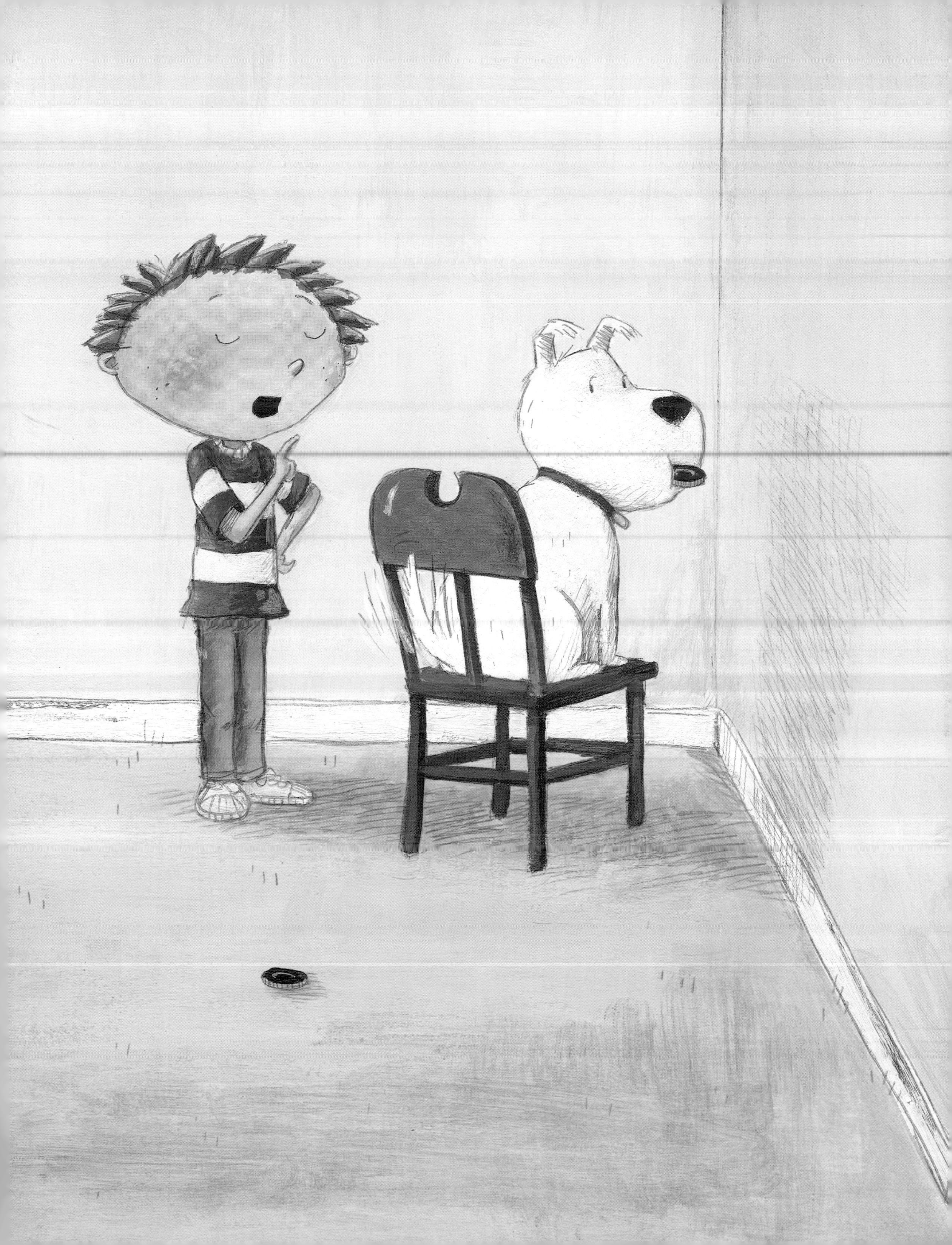

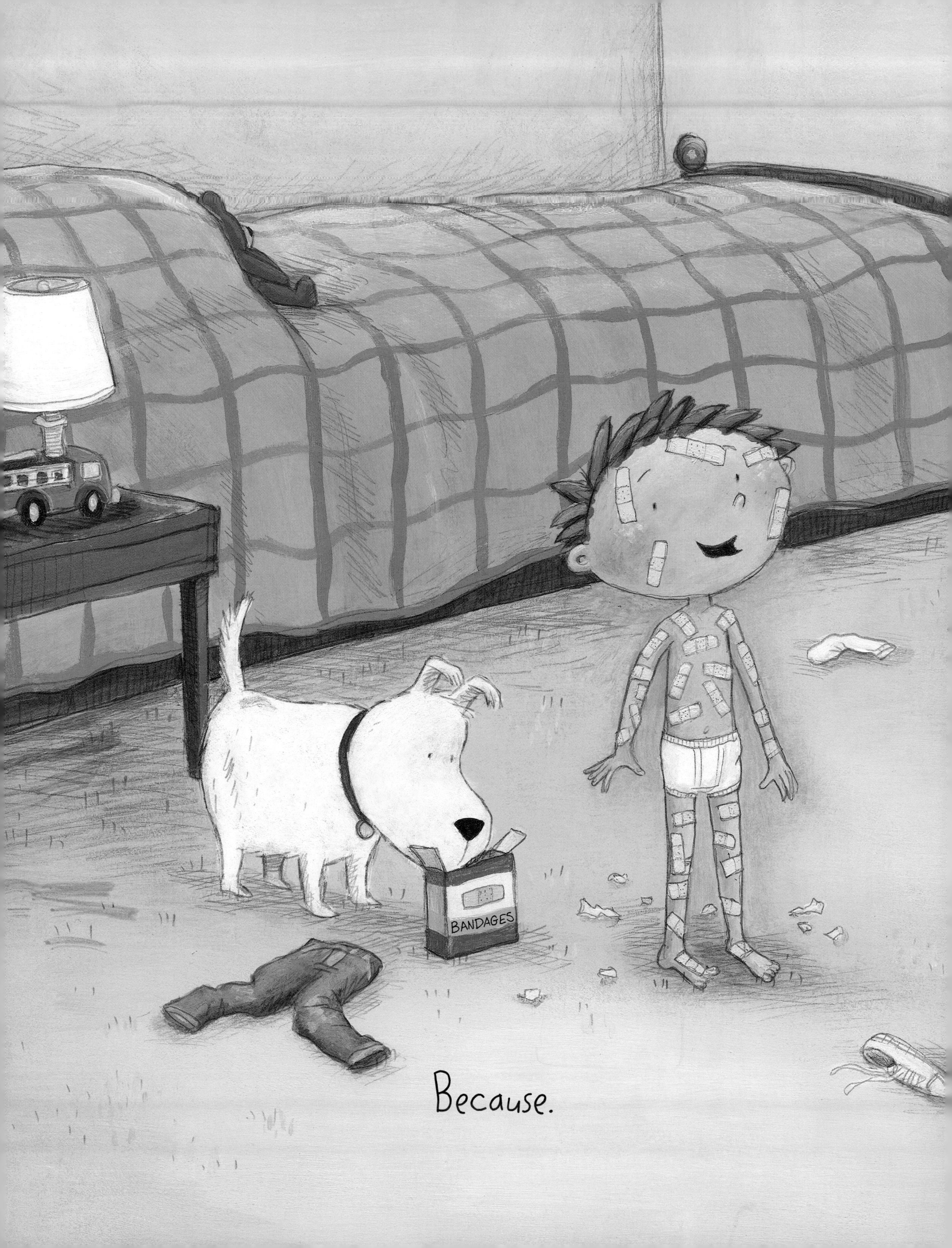
BANDAGES

Because.

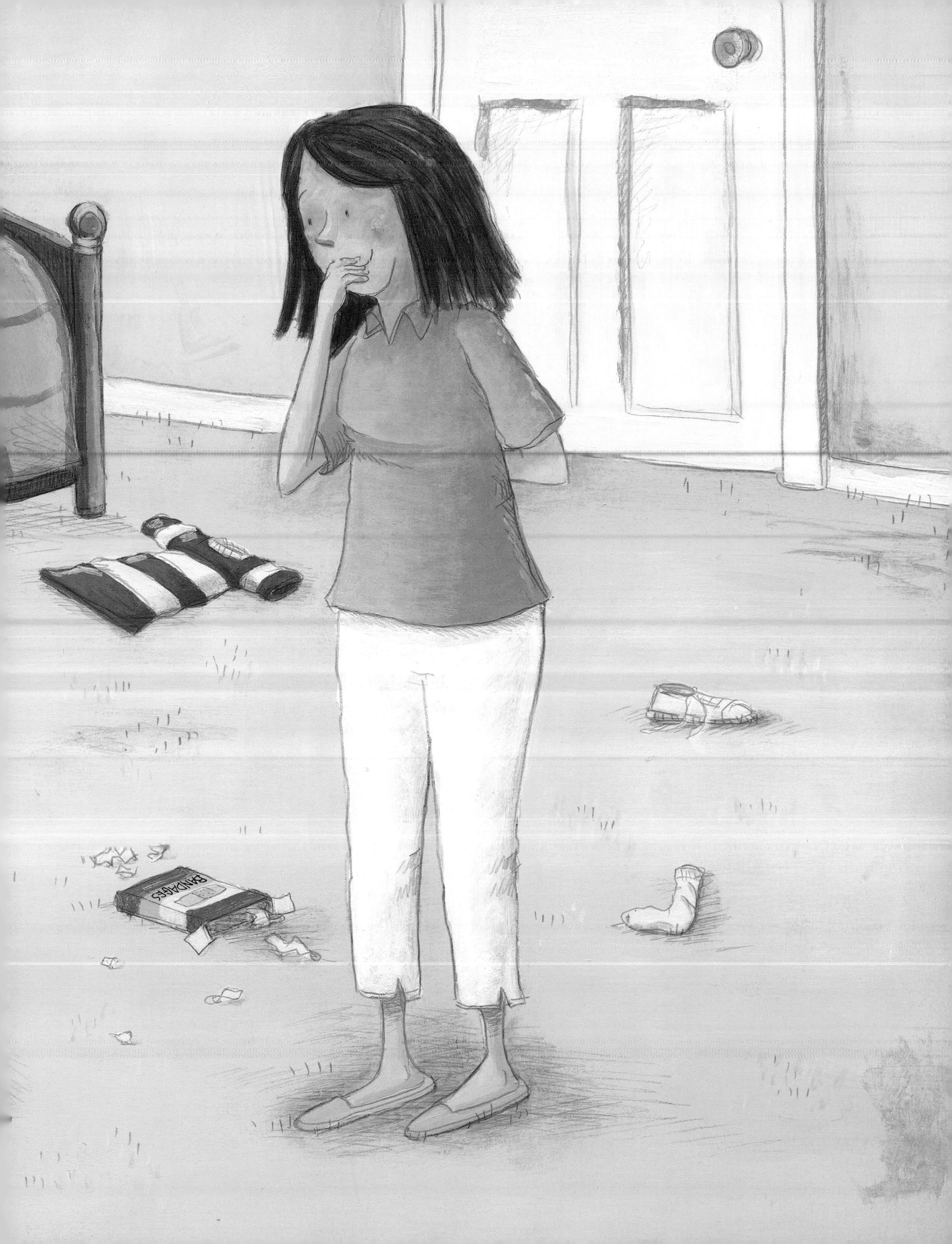
BANDAGES

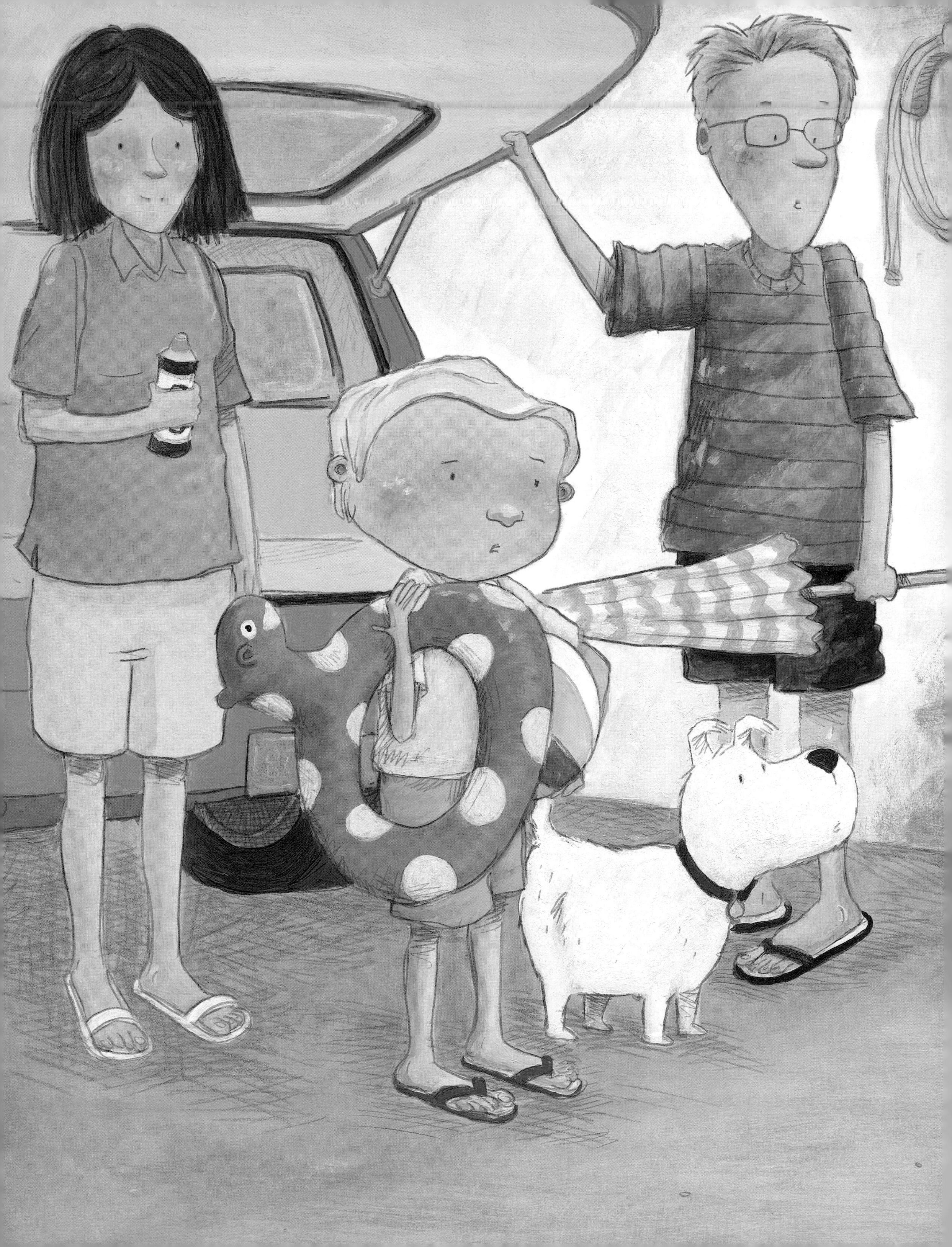

Because I might need it!

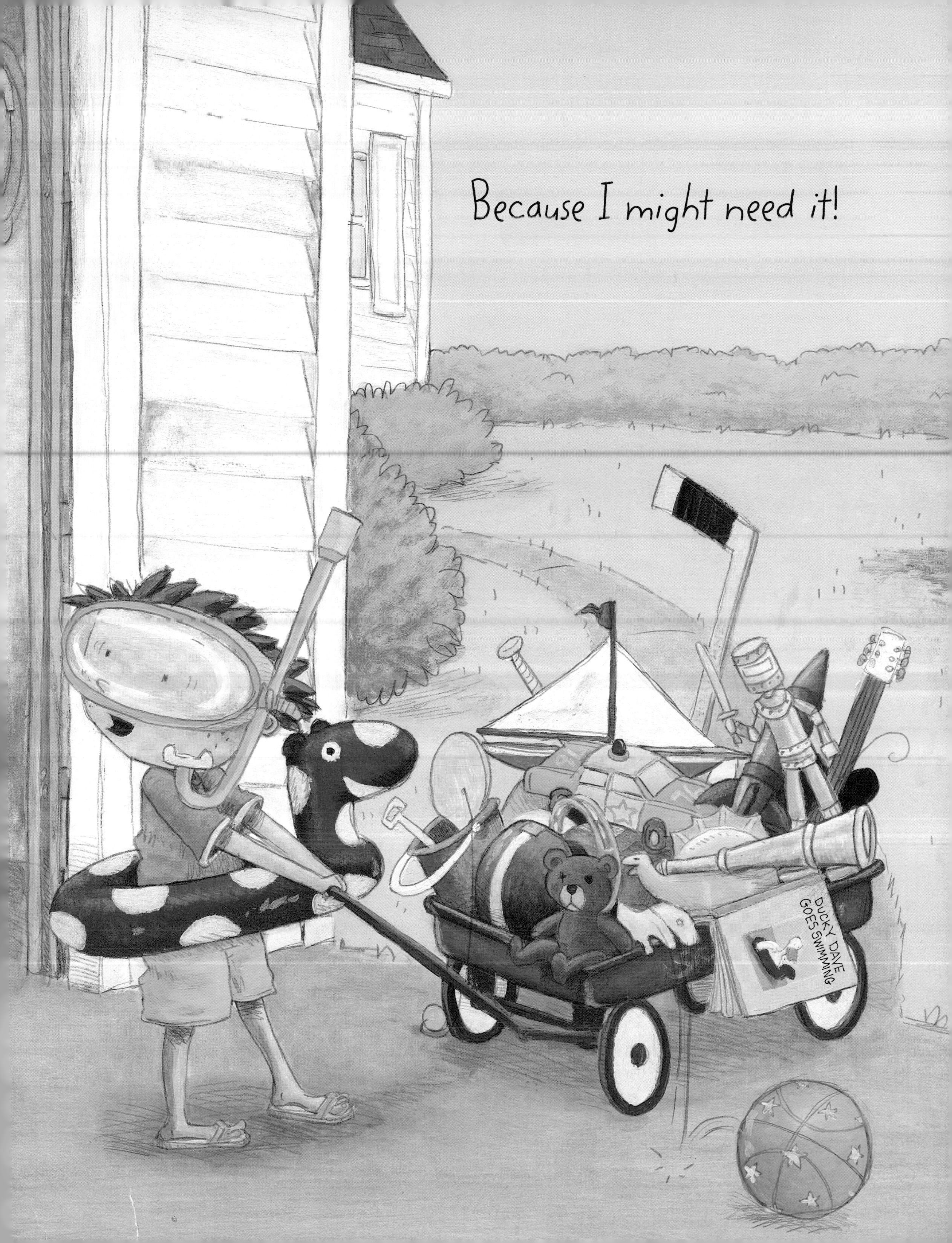
DUCKY DAVE
GOES SWIMMING

Because you're hogging all the space.

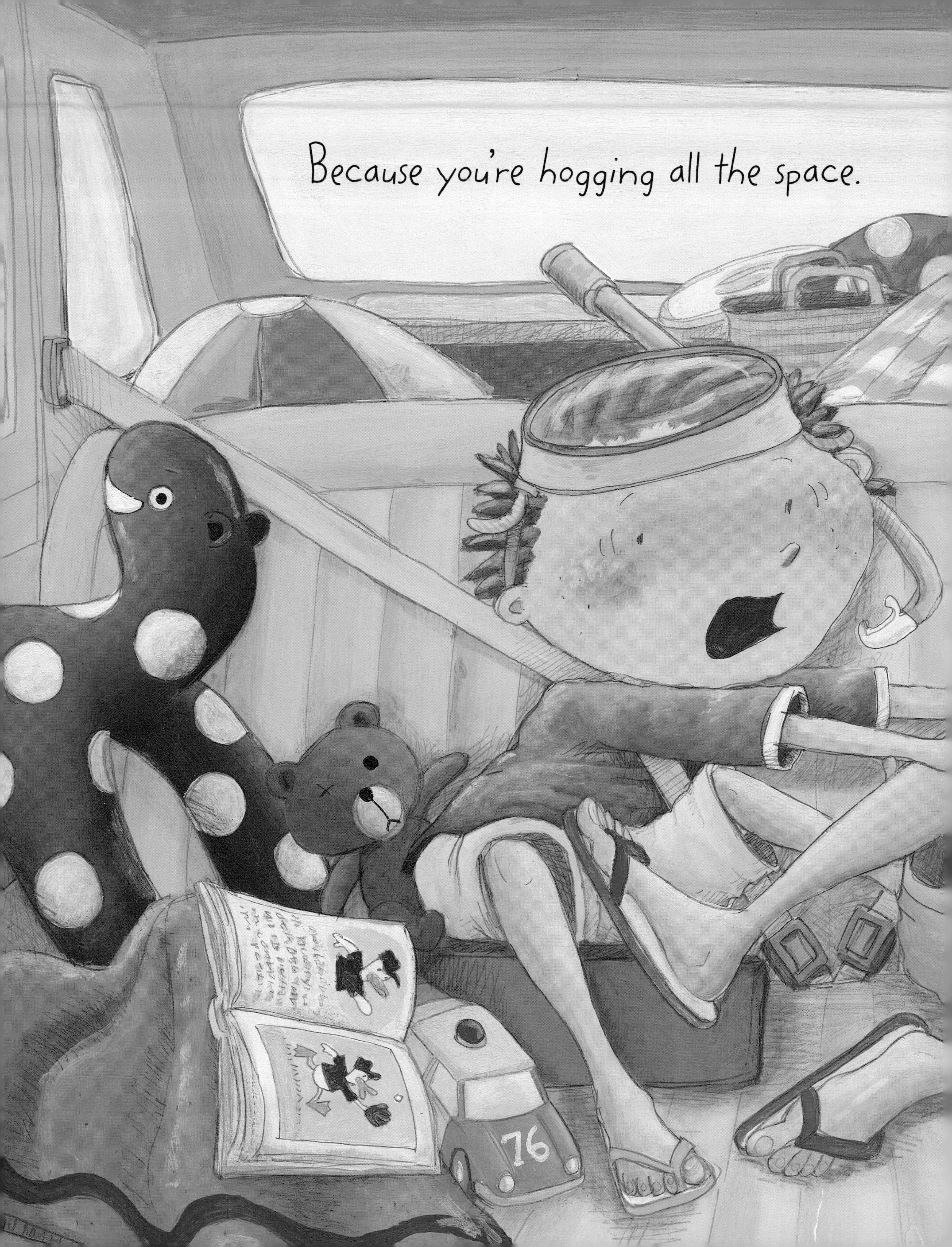
76

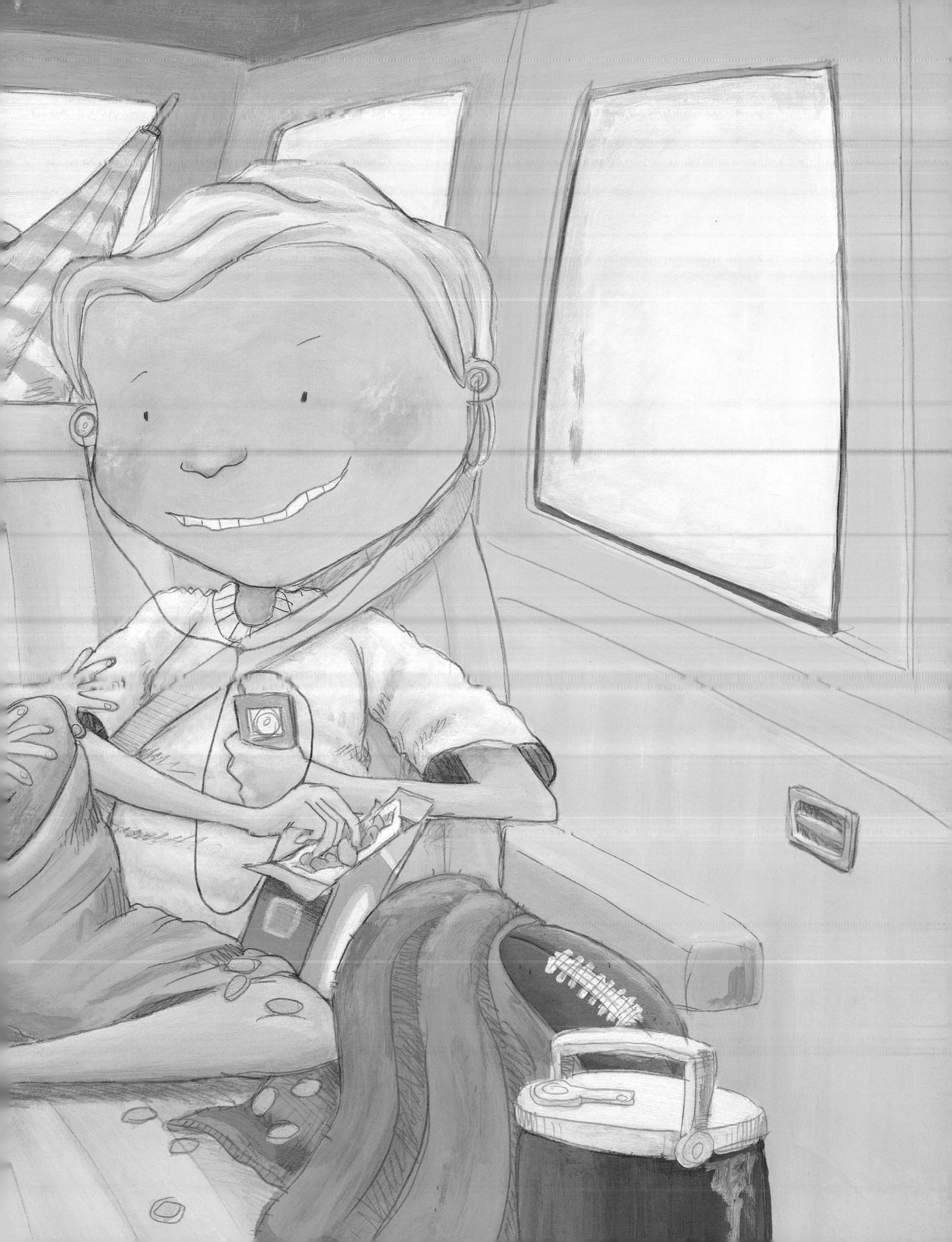

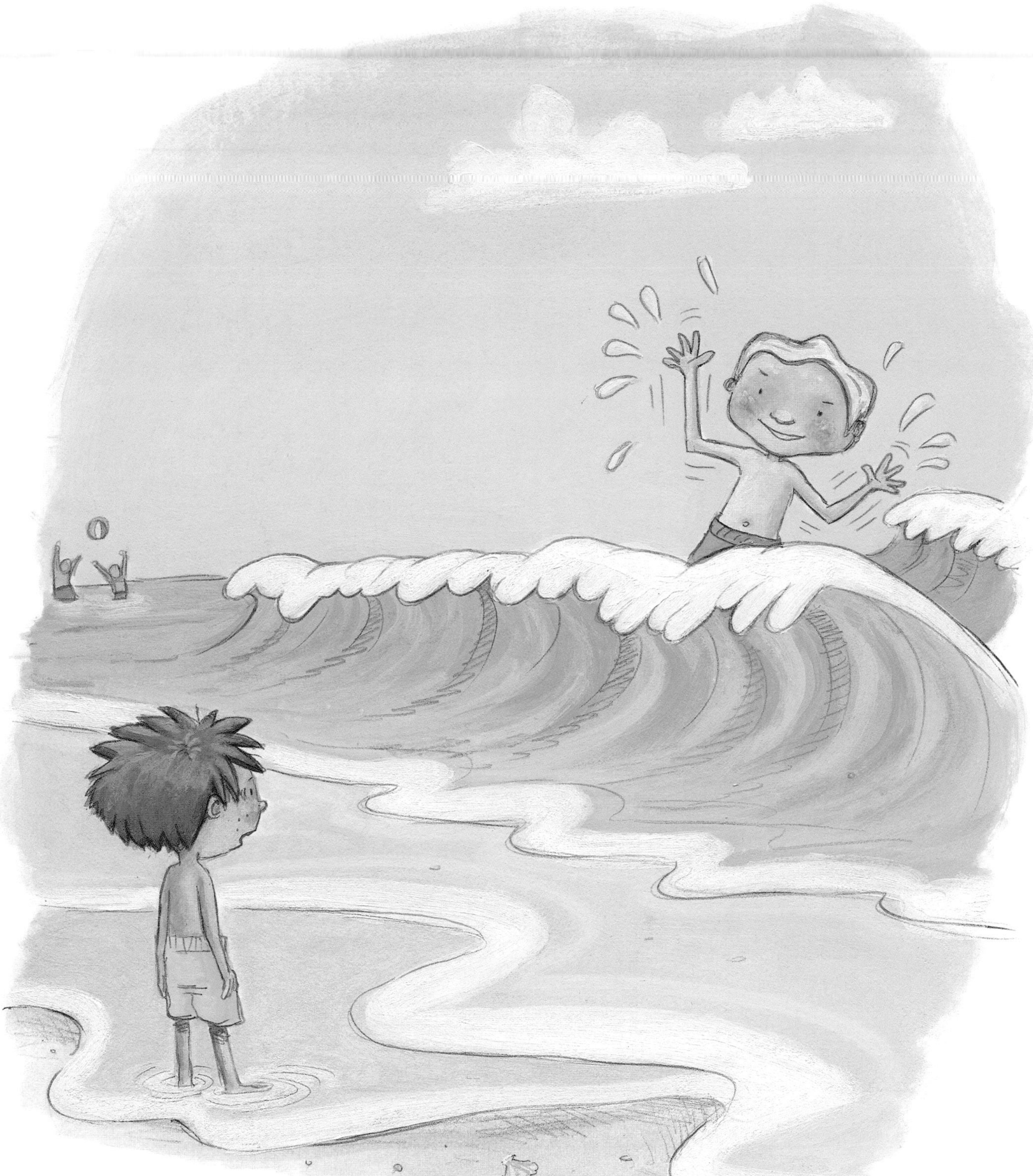

Because you're big and I'm little.

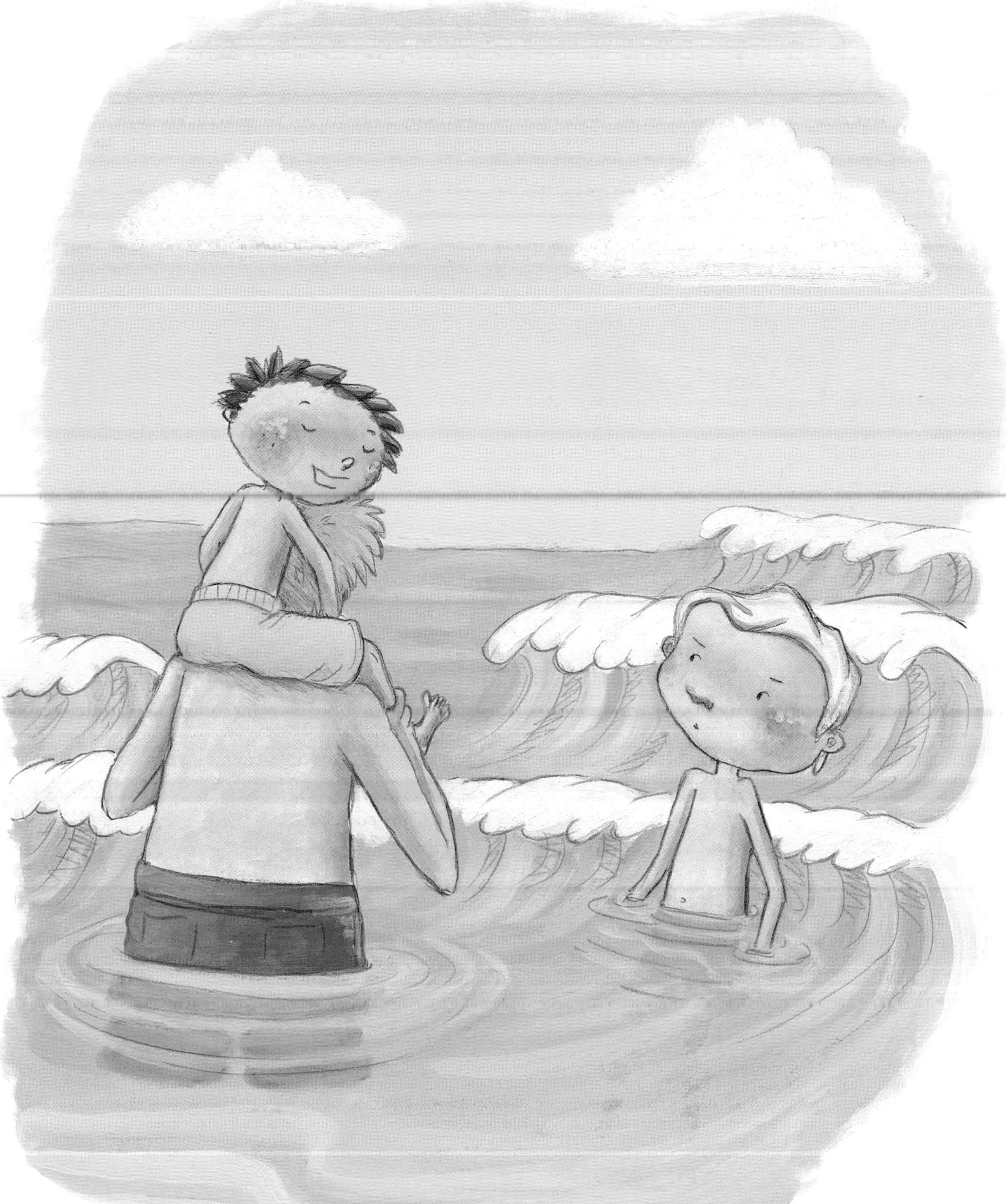

Because I'm little and you're big.

Because we're hungry!

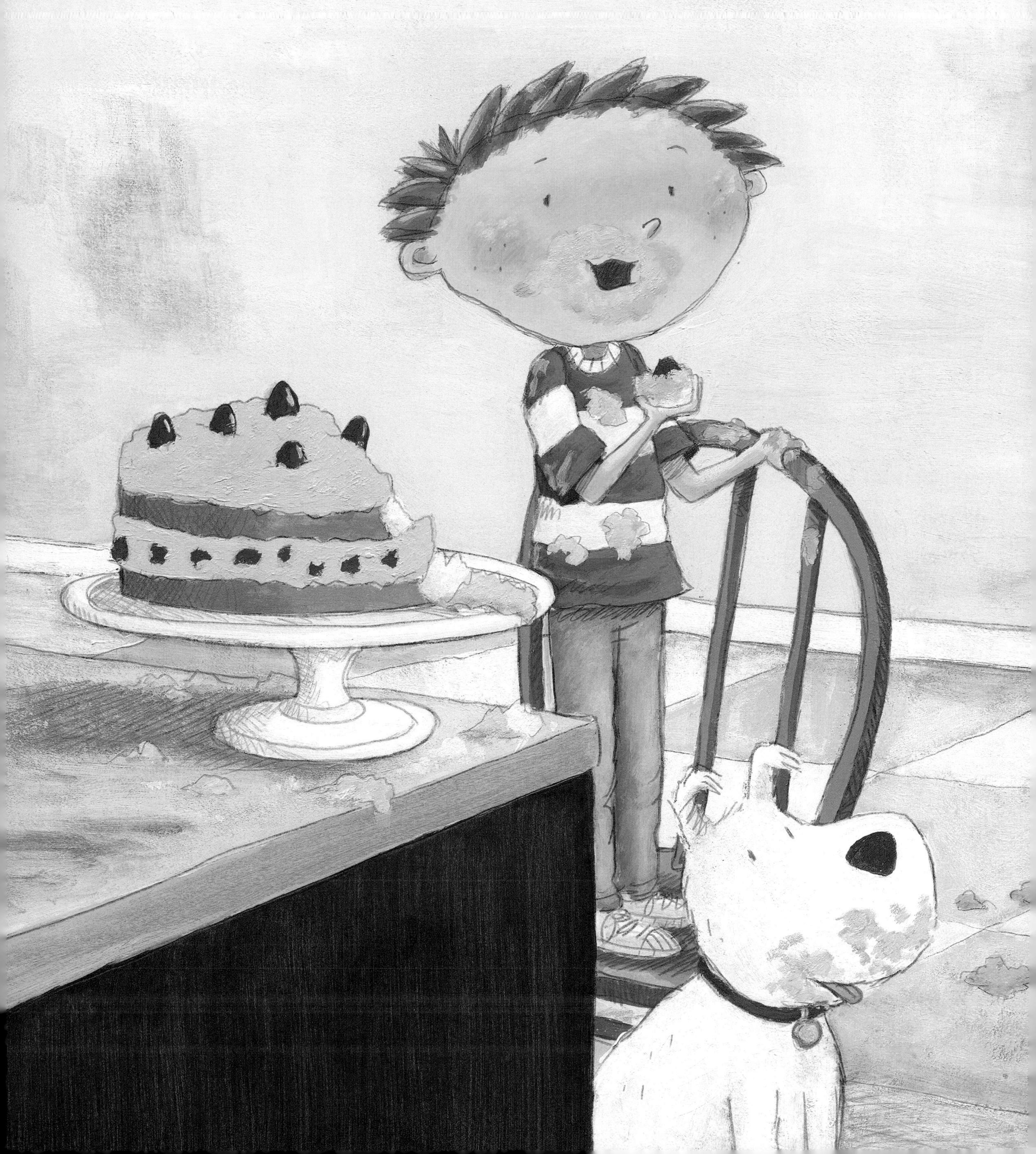

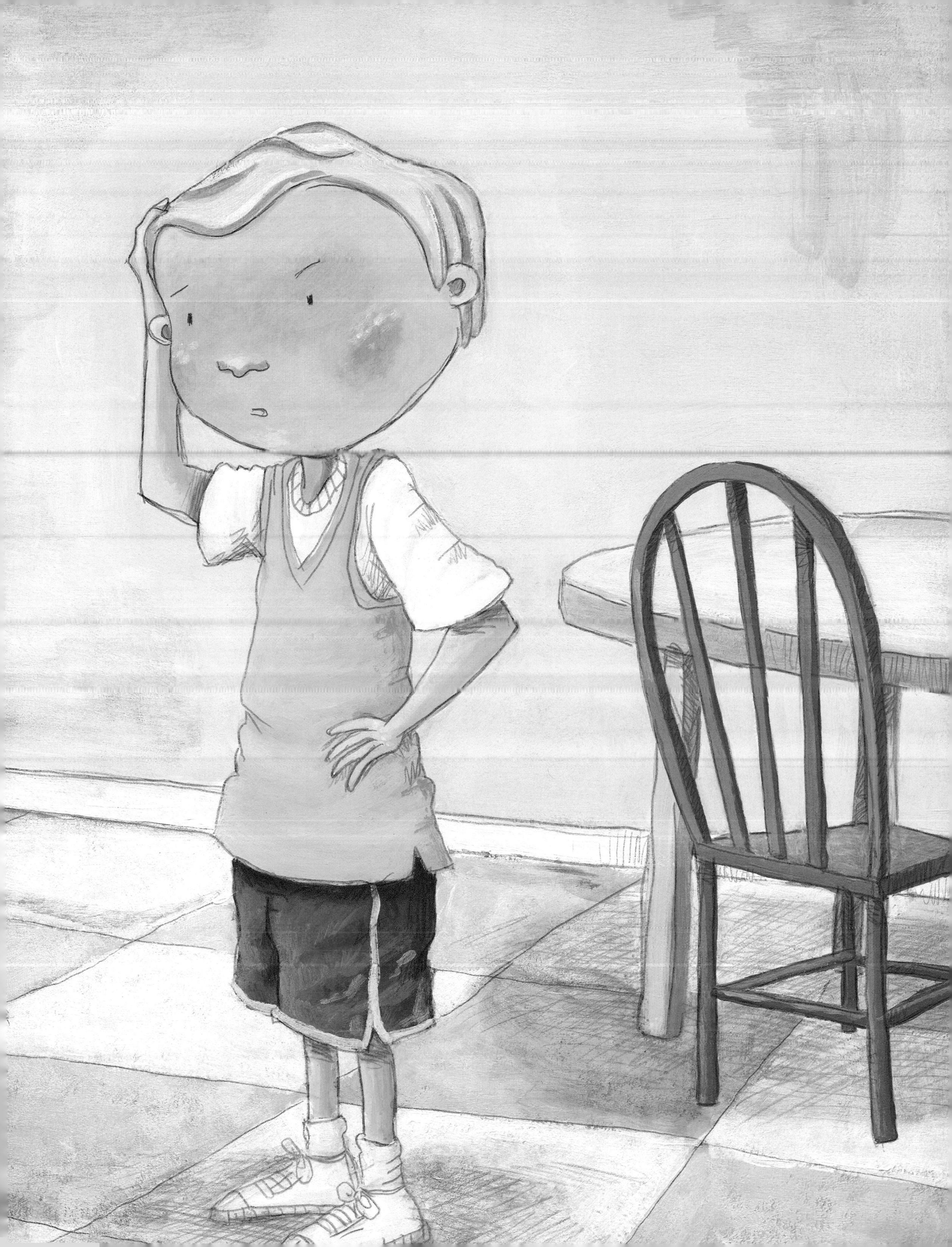

Because.

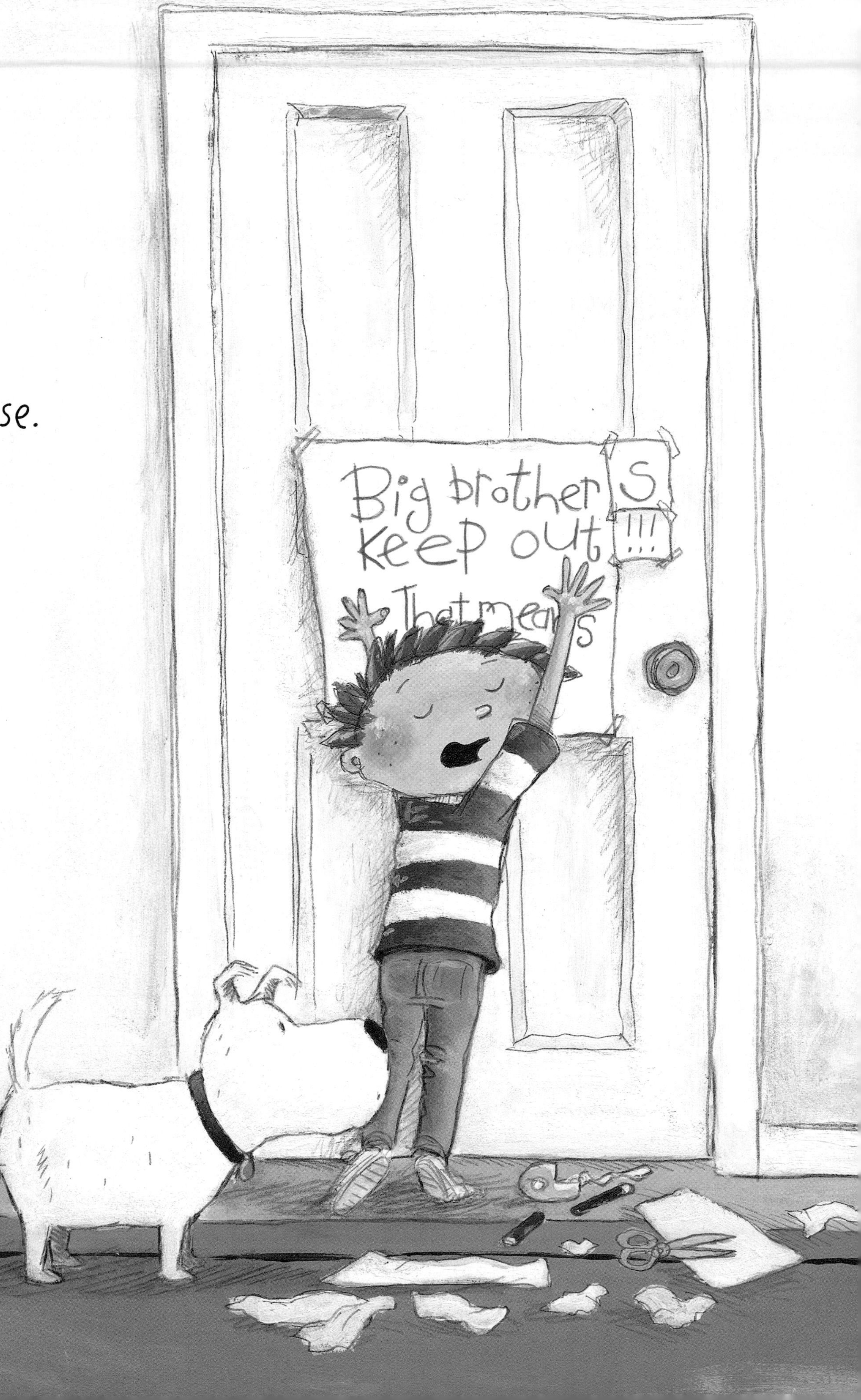
Big brother S
Keep out !!!

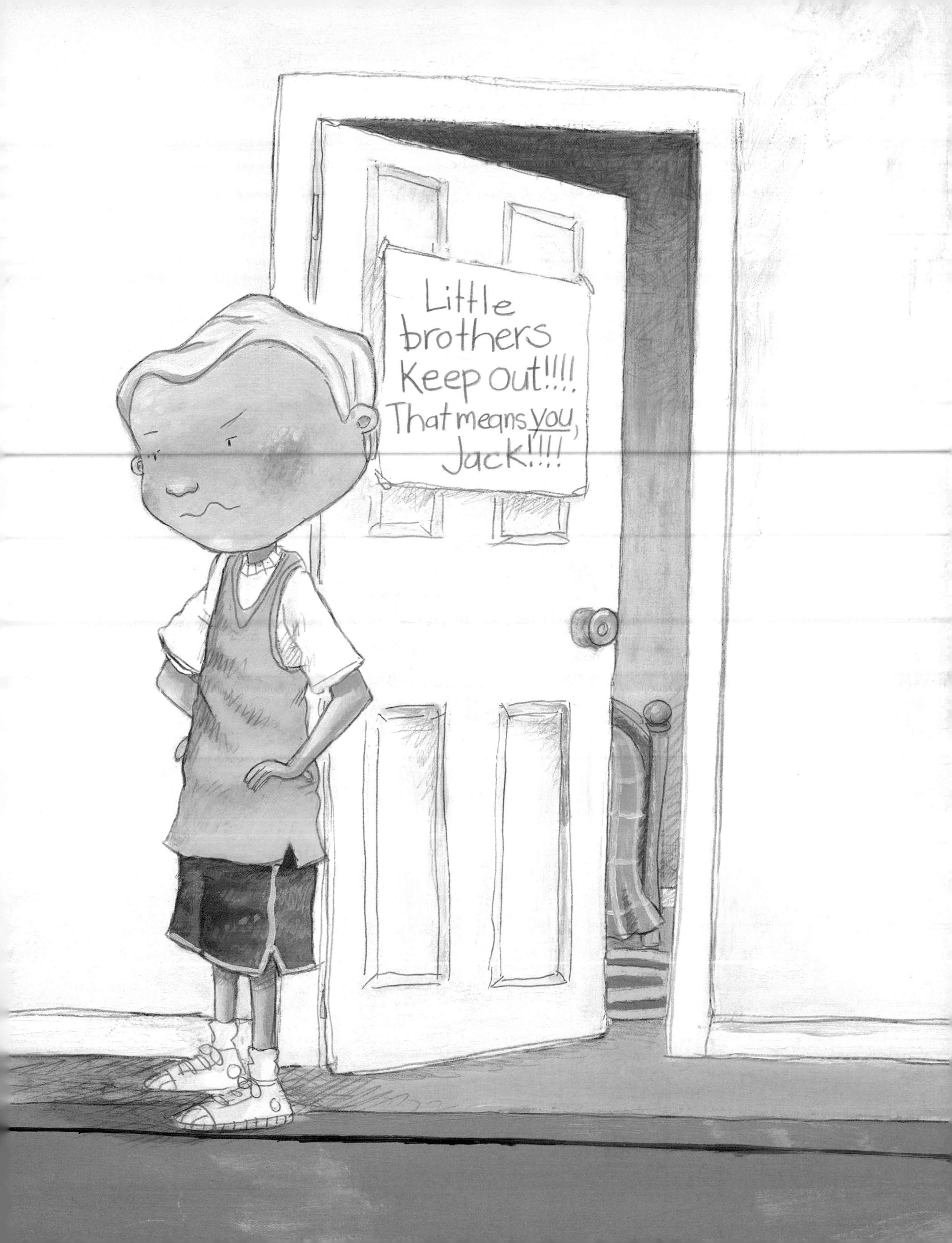
Little
brothers
Keep out!!!!
That means you,
Jack!!!!

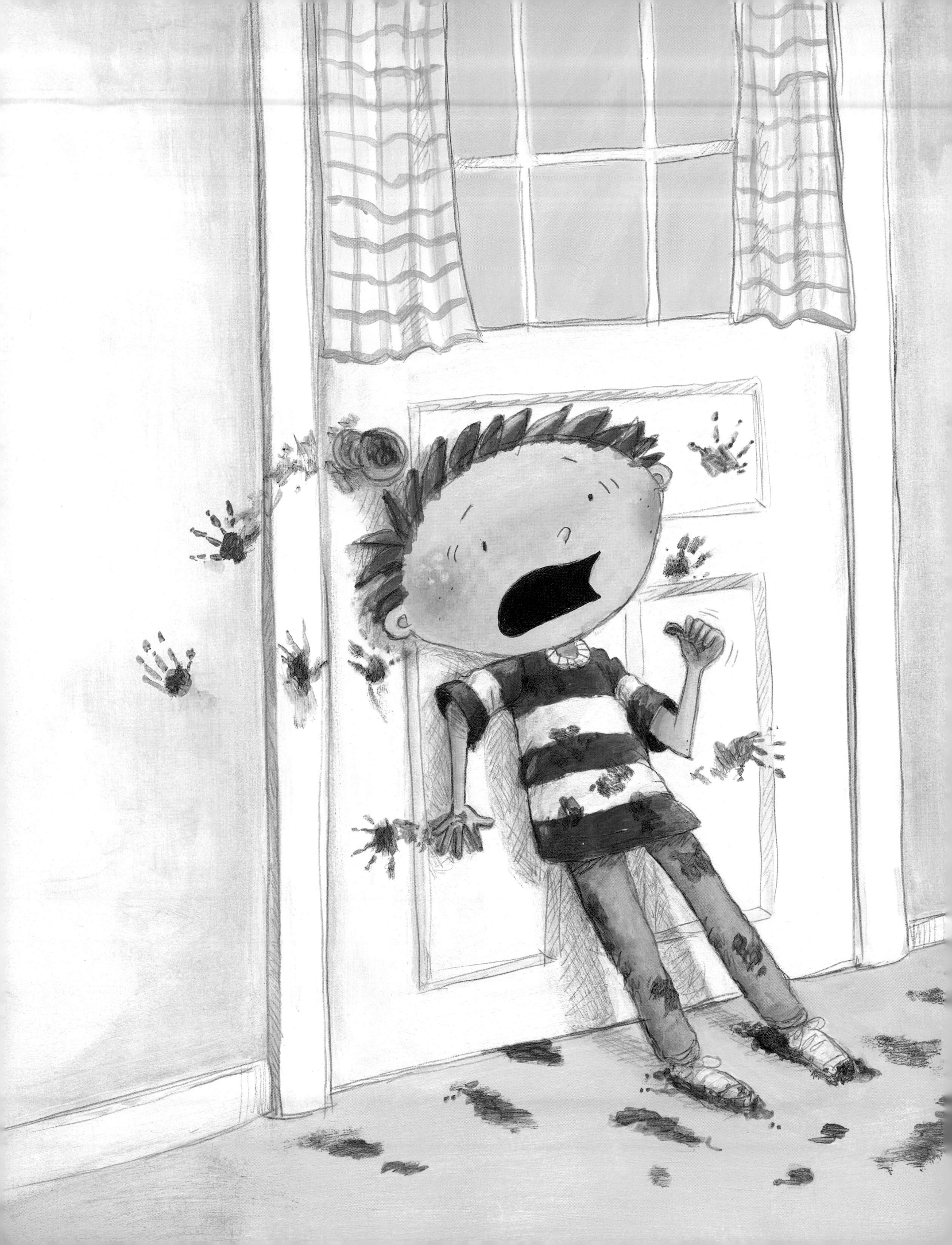

Because a bee is
trying to get us!

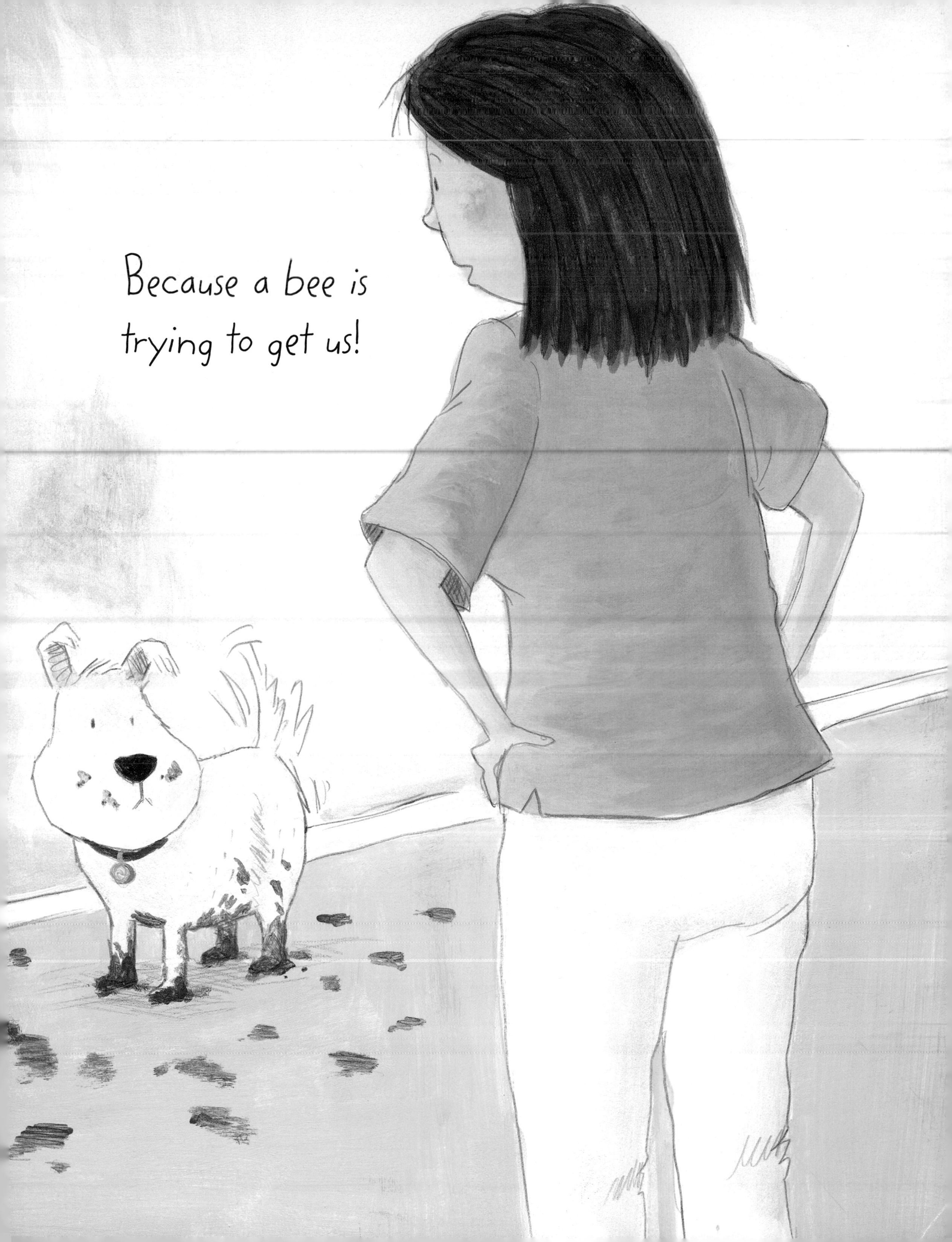

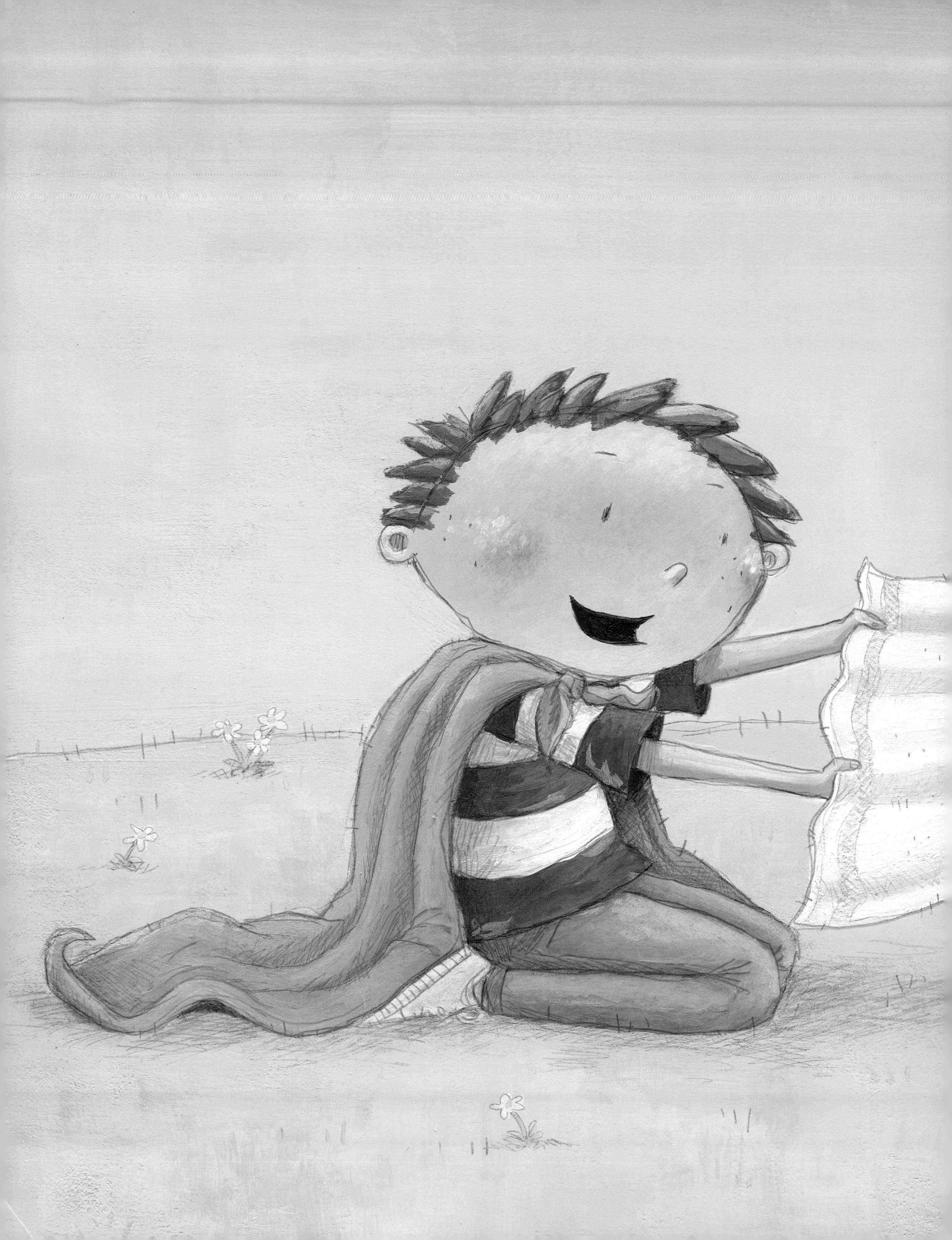

Because you need it to fly.

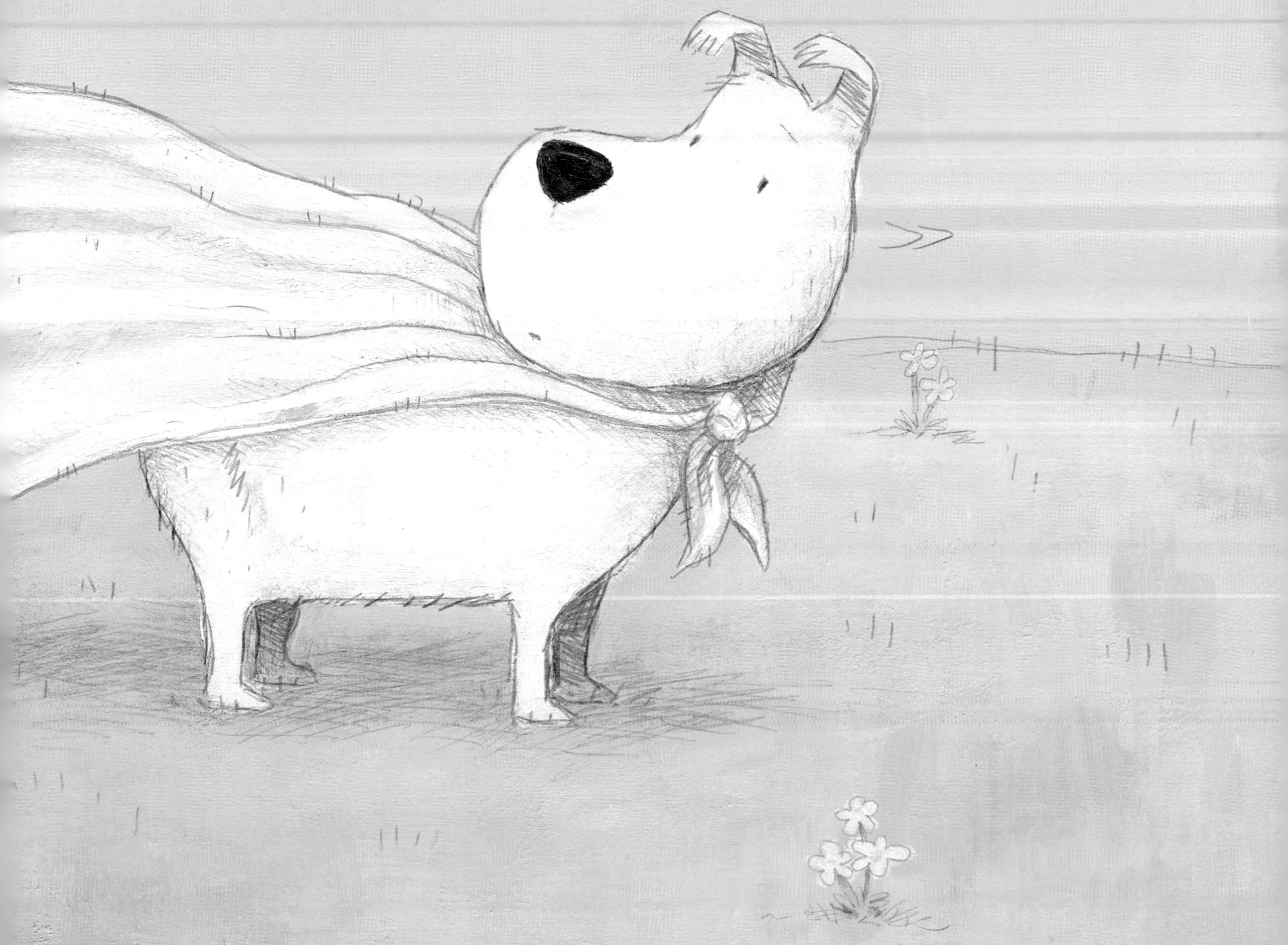

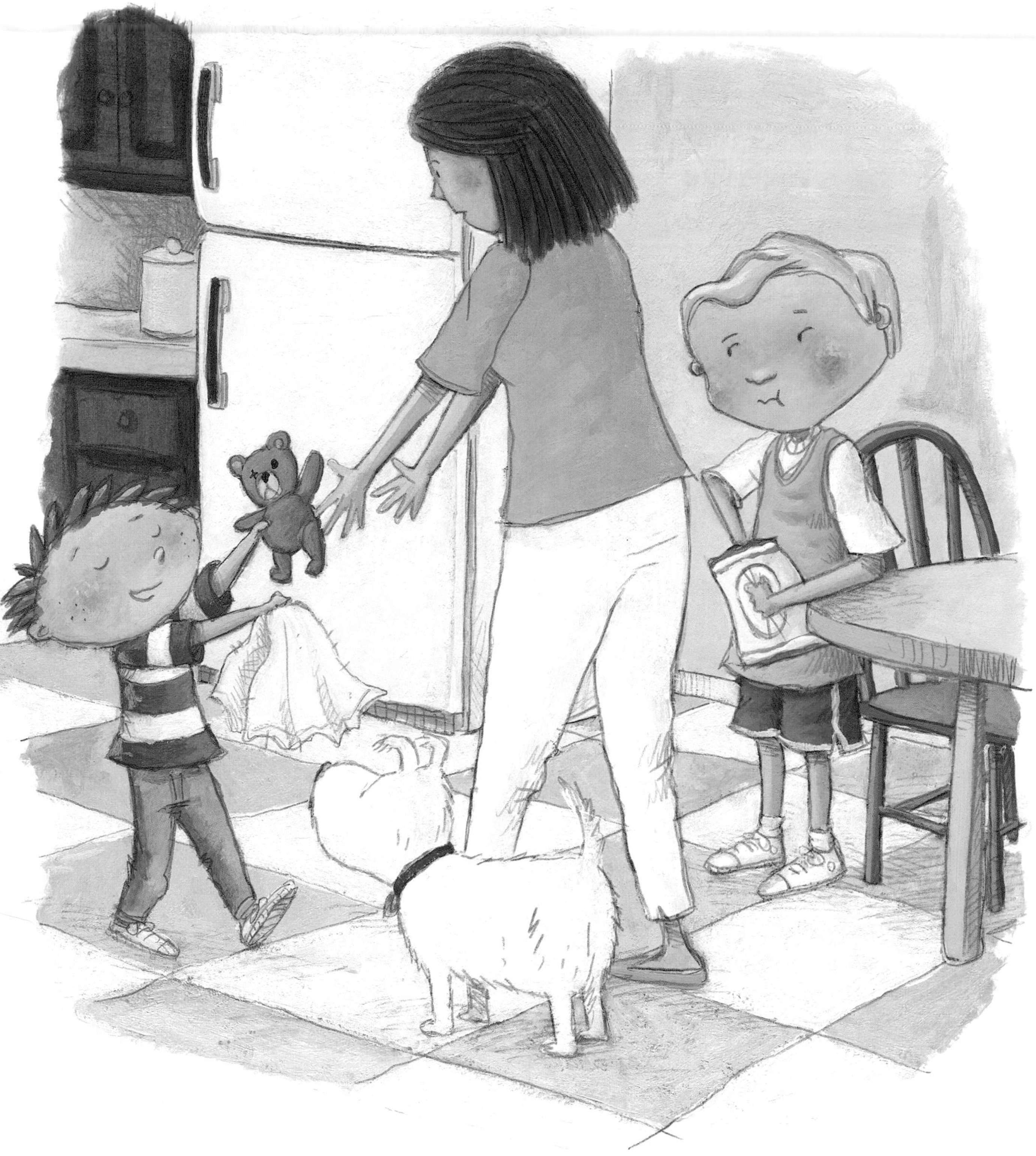

Because I'm almost grown up.

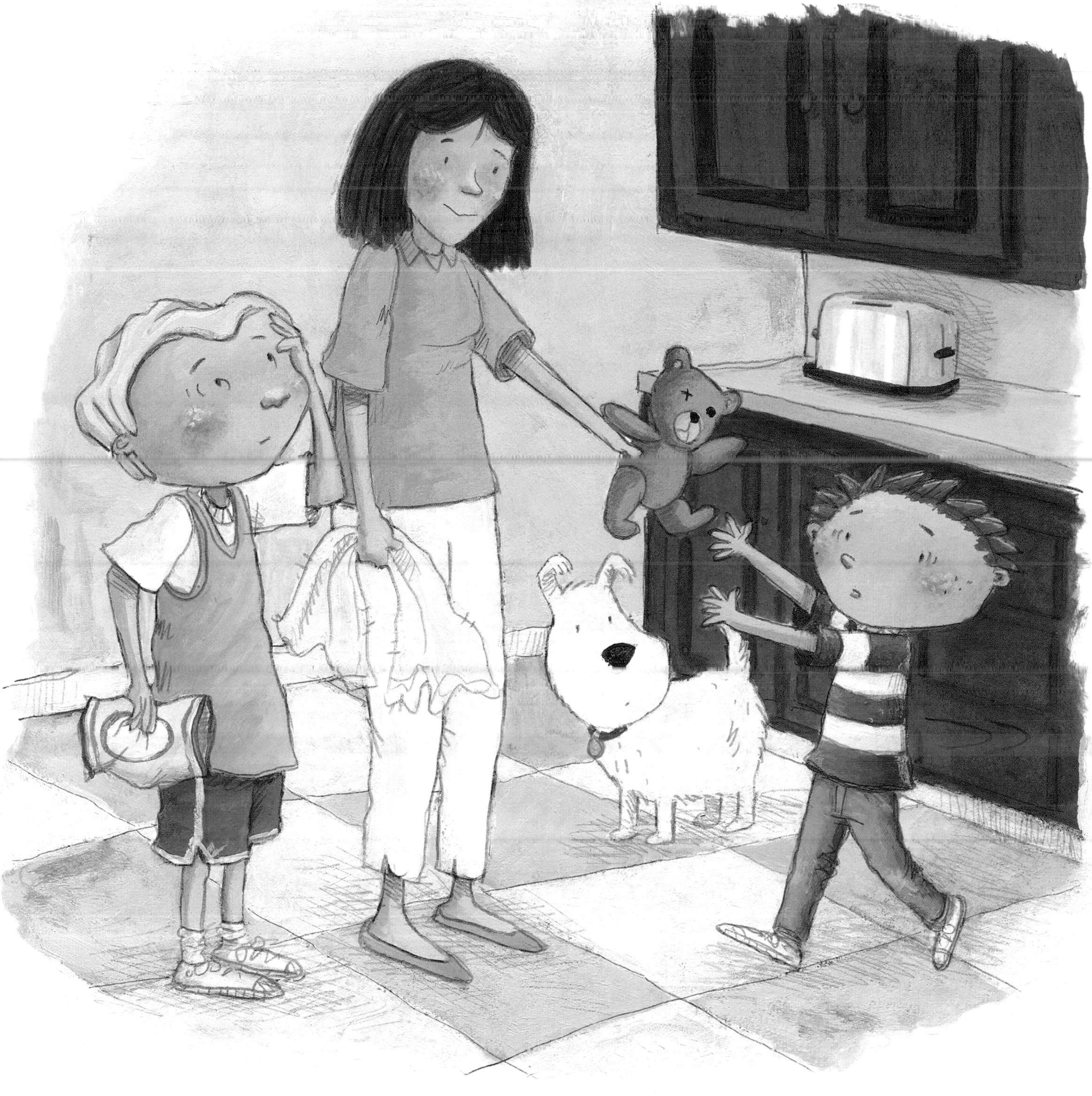

Because he needs me.

Because sometimes I have to play
with my other friends.

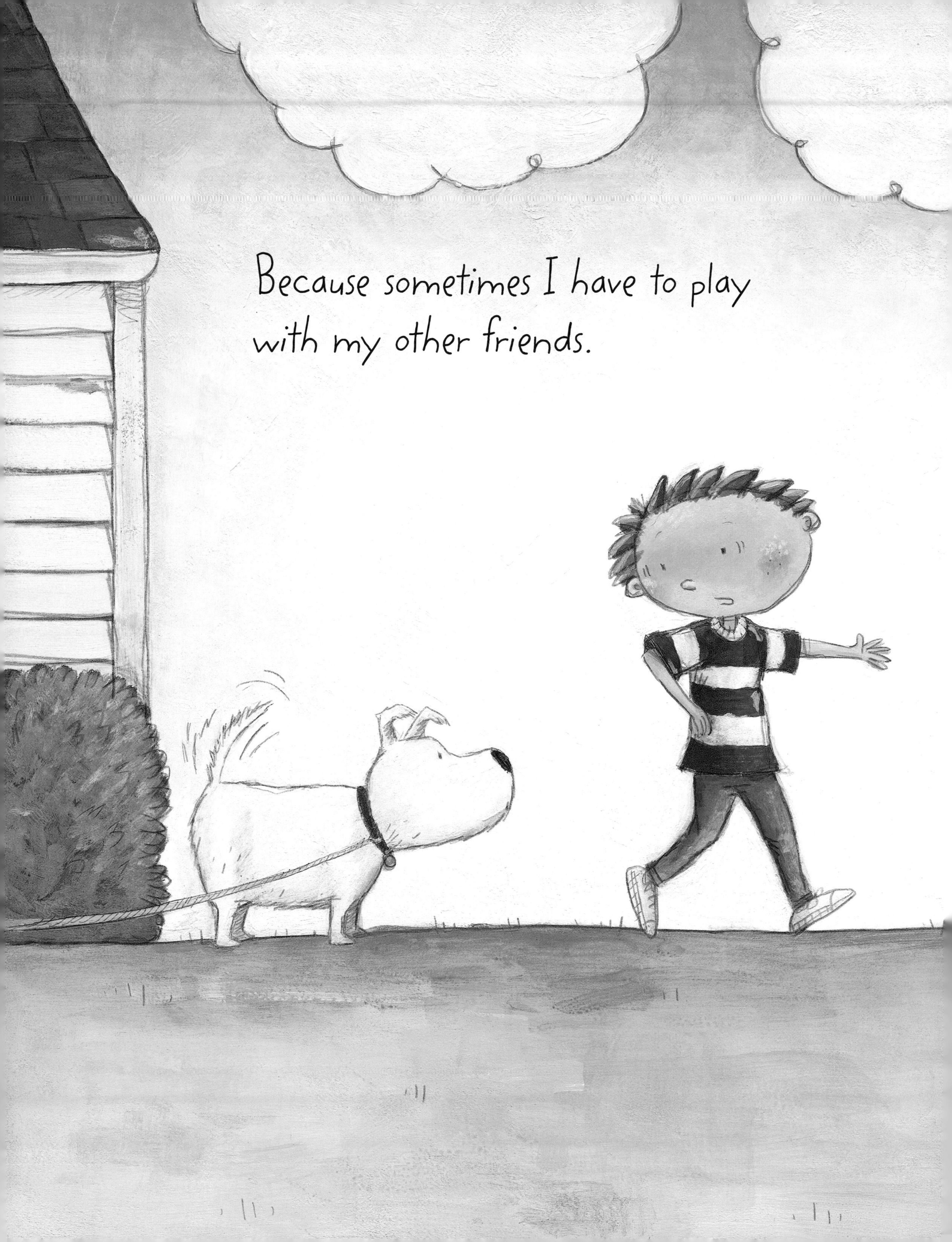

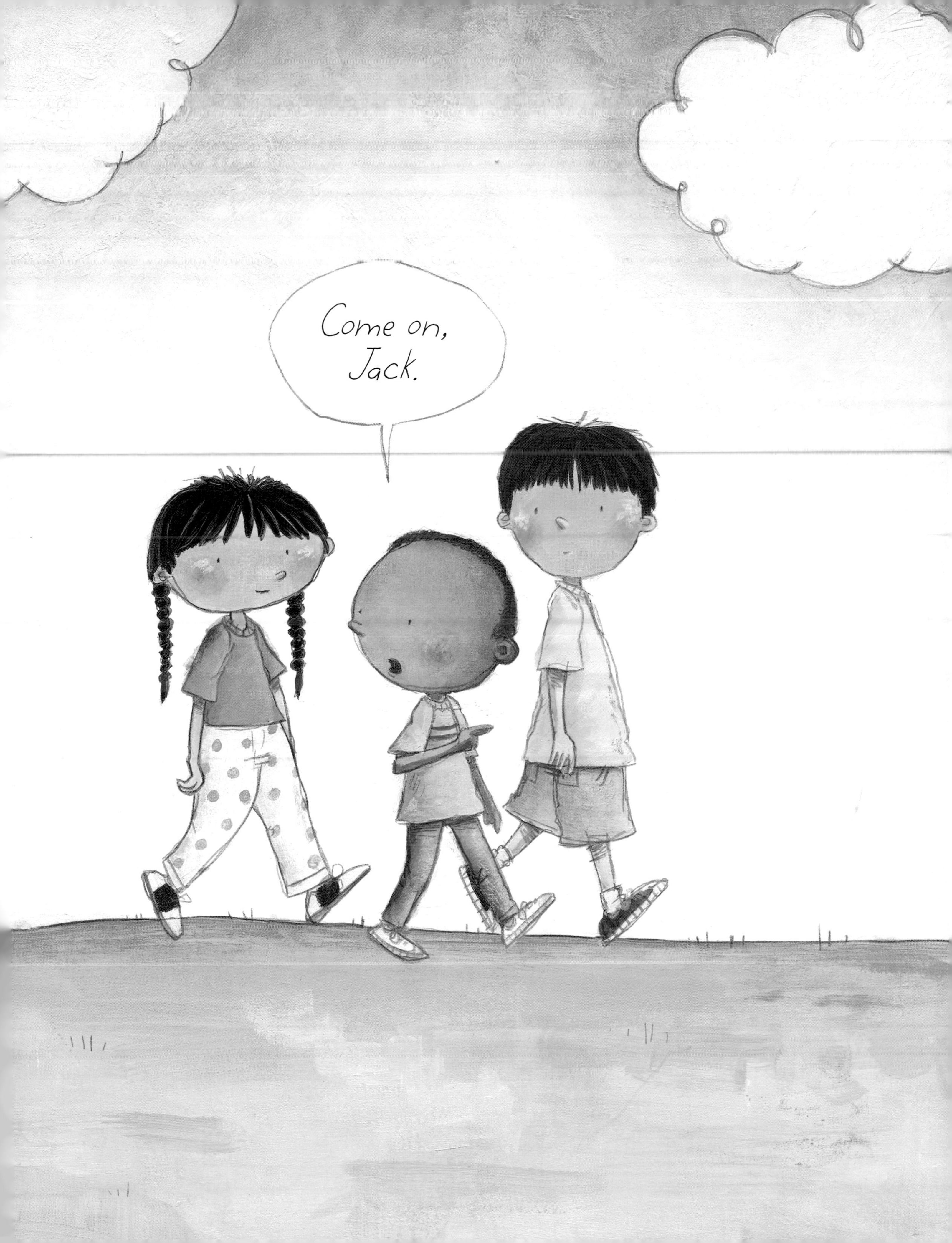
Come on,
Jack.

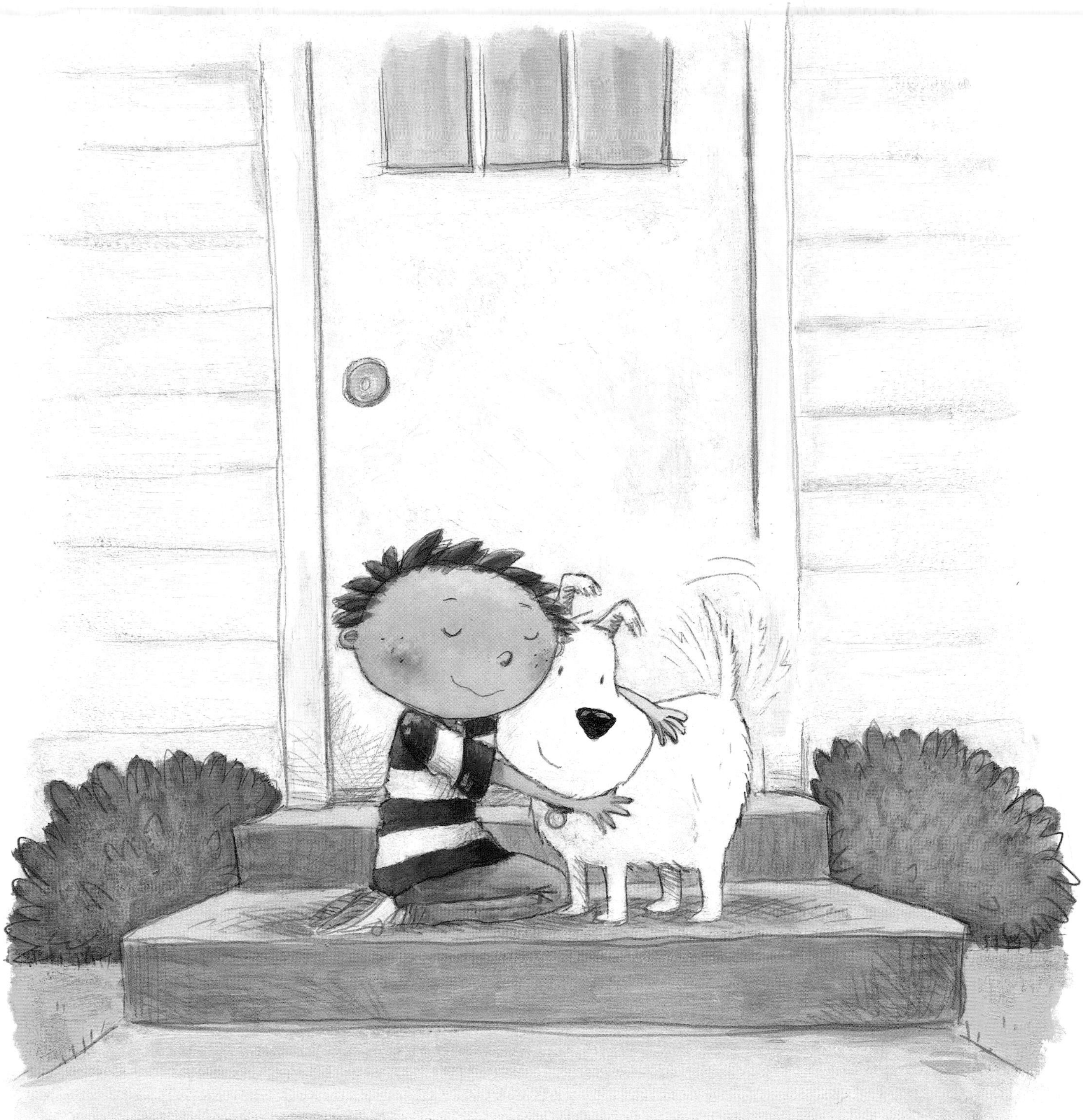

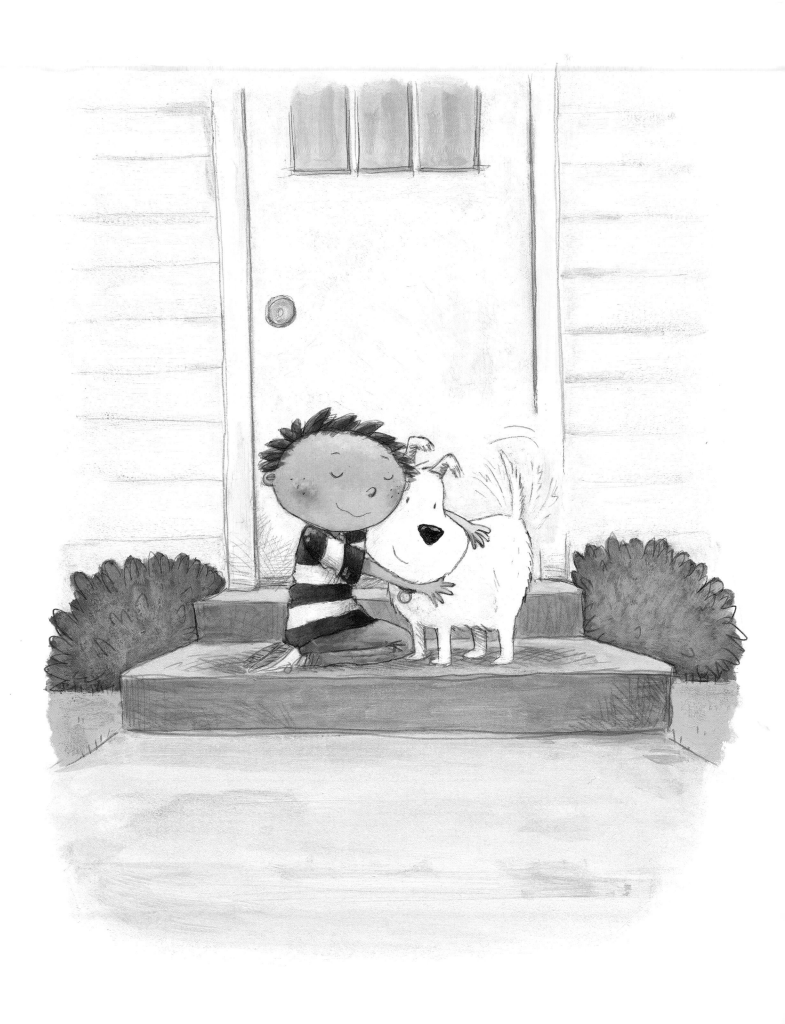

Just because.

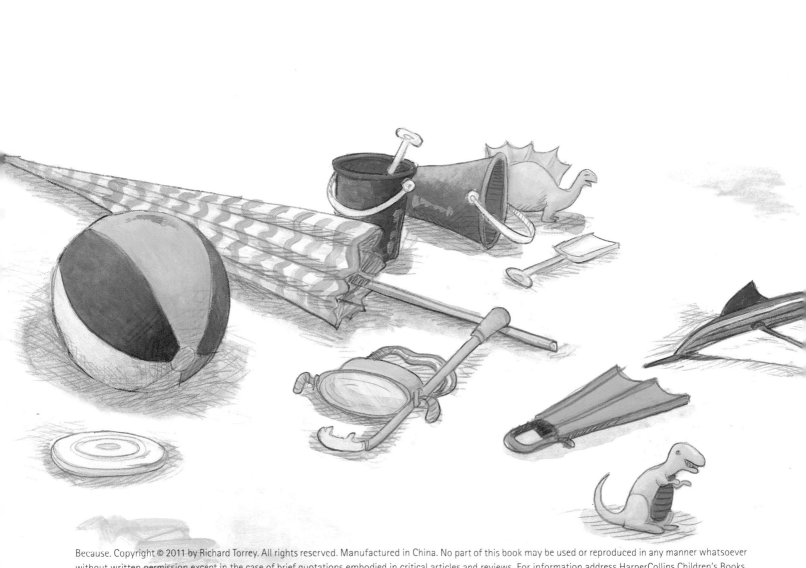

For information address HarperCollins Children's Books, a division of HarperCollins Publishers, 10 East 53rd Street, New York, NY 10022. www.harpercollinschildrens.com.
Library of Congress Cataloging-in-Publication Data Torrey, Rich. Because / Richard Torrey. – 1st ed. p. cm. Summary: A little boy argues that "because" is a perfectly acceptable response to a question, in spite of what his mother says. ISBN 978-0-06-156173-3 (trade bdg. : alk. paper) – ISBN 978-0-06-156178-8 (lib. bdg. : alk. paper) [1. Behavior–Fiction.] I. Title. PZ7.T64573Bl 2011 [E]–dc22 2010010510 CIP AC
Typography by Dana Fritts. 11 12 13 14 15 SCP 10 9 8 7 6 5 4 3 2 1 ❖ First Edition